HER RODEO MAN

BY
CATHY McDAVID

MILLS & BOON

Published in Great Britain 2015
by Mills & Boon, an imprint of Harlequin (UK) Limited,
Eton House, 18-24 Paradise Road, Richmond, Surrey, TW9 1SR

© 2015 Cathy McDavid

ISBN: 978-0-263-25123-4

23-0315

Harlequin (UK) Limited's policy is to use papers that are natural, renewable and recyclable products and made from wood grown in sustainable forests. The logging and manufacturing processes conform to the legal environmental regulations of the country of origin.

Printed and bound in Spain
by CPI, Barcelona

For the past eighteen years **Cathy McDavid** has been juggling a family, a job and writing, and doing pretty well at it, except for the housecleaning part. "Mostly" retired from the corporate business world, she writes full-time from her home in Scottsdale, Arizona, near the breathtaking McDowell Mountains. Her twins have "mostly" left home, returning every now and then to raid her refrigerators. On weekends, she heads to her cabin in the mountains, always taking her laptop with her. You can visit her website at www.cathymcdavid.com.

To Mike…and the incredible spark you always ignite.
Here's to forever, my love.

Chapter One

The day Ryder Beckett swore would never come had arrived. He'd returned to Reckless, Arizona, and the Easy Money Rodeo Arena. But instead of a hero's welcome, he was slinking home like a scolded puppy with his tail tucked firmly between his legs.

Really slinking. He should be meeting his father in the arena office. In fact, he was five minutes late. Only, Ryder had continued walking. Around the main barn, past the row of outdoor horse stalls, all the way to the horse pastures. There he stopped and forced himself to draw a long breath.

He did want to be here, he told himself. Though, to be honest, he needed to be here. Be somewhere, anyway. Why not Reckless, where he could maybe, possibly, mend a bridge or two? He would if his baby sister, Liberty, had her way. For Ryder, the jury was still out.

Keeping a low profile. Yeah, he decided, that had a better ring to it than slinking. Then again, Ryder possessed a talent for putting a positive spin on things. It was what had propelled him to the top in his field. Stupidity was what led to his downfall.

As he stood at the pasture fence, his leather dress shoes sank deep into the soft dirt. He'd have a chore cleaning them later. At the moment, he didn't care.

When, he absently wondered, was the last time he'd worn a pair of boots? Or ridden a horse, for that matter? The answer came quickly. Five years ago during his last strained visit. He'd sworn then and there he'd never set sight on Reckless again. The aftermath of another falling-out with his mother.

Recent events had altered the circumstance of their enduring disagreement. Liberty, the one most hurt by their mother's lies, had managed to make peace with both their parents. Not so Ryder. His anger at their mother's betrayal hadn't dimmed one bit in the twenty-five years since she'd divorced their father.

Was coming home a mistake? Only time would tell. In any case, he wasn't staying long.

In the pasture, a woman haltered a large black pony and led it slowly toward the gate. Other horses, a half dozen or so pregnant mares, ambled behind, bobbing their heads and swishing their tails. Whatever might be happening, they wanted in on it.

Ryder leaned his forearms on the top fence railing. Even at this distance, he could tell two things: the pony was severely lame, and the woman was spectacularly attractive. Both drew his attention, and, for the moment, his meeting with his father was forgotten.

The two were a study in contrast. While the pony hobbled painfully, favoring its front left foot, the woman moved with elegance and grace, her long black hair misbehaving in the mild breeze. She stopped frequently to check on the pony and, when she did, rested her hand affectionately on its sleek neck.

Something about her struck a familiar, but elusive, chord with him. Who was she? A memory teased at the fringes of his mind but remained out of reach.

As he watched, the knots of tension residing in his shoulders relaxed. That was until she changed direction and headed toward him. Then, he immediately perked up, and his senses went on high alert.

"Hi," she said as she approached. "Can I help you?"

She was even prettier up close. Large dark eyes analyzed him with unapologetic interest from a model-perfect oval face. Her full mouth stretched into a warm smile impossible not to return. The red T-shirt tucked into a pair of well-worn jeans emphasized her long legs and slim waist.

"I'm meeting someone." He didn't add that he was now ten minutes late or that the someone was, in fact, his father.

"Oh. Okay." She took him in with a glance that said it all. Visitors to the Easy Money didn't usually wear suits and ties.

"Mercer Beckett," Ryder said.

"He's in the office, I think."

"That's what he told me."

At the gate, she paused and tilted her head, her gaze shifting from mild interest to open curiosity. "Can I show you the way?"

"Thanks. I already know it."

"You've been here before?"

"You…could say that. But it's been a while."

"Well, welcome back."

That smile again, familiar but not, and most appealing. It was almost enough to make Ryder break his promise to himself to steer clear of work romances. He'd learned that lesson the hard way and had paid the price with his now defunct career.

Not that he'd be working with this woman exactly. But she was probably a customer of the Becketts, one who boarded her pony at the arena. Close enough.

"You should fire your farrier and find another one." Ryder nodded at the pony. "He or she isn't worth a lick."

The woman's brows arched in surprise and emphasized their elegant shape. "I beg your pardon?"

He indicated the pony's right front hoof. "She has a contracted heel. From incorrect shoeing."

"No offense intended, but you don't exactly strike me as an expert."

"I'm not. But I do have some experience." Living, breathing, eating and sleeping horses for the first half of his life. "You pull that shoe off, and you'll see an immediate improvement."

"Could be laminitis," she countered. "That's common in ponies."

"It's not laminitis."

"You sound sure."

"Remove the shoe, and you'll see." When she hesitated, he added, "What could it hurt?"

"I'll ask one of the hands." She slid the latch and opened the gate.

"I can do it for you. Remove the shoe."

"In those clothes?"

"What's a little dirt?"

She laughed, a low, sexy sound he quite liked. "We'll see."

Was he crazy? Flirting with a potential customer. A woman who could be married with three kids, for all he knew.

She started through the gate, leading the pony. The horses behind her also wanted out and began shoving their way into the narrow opening. A bottleneck formed, with the more aggressive of the horses squealing and nipping at their neighbors.

"Back now." The woman waved a hand, which had almost no effect.

Ryder stepped forward. If the horses succeeded in getting loose, the Easy Money hands would be in for a merry chase.

"I'll help."

Before she could object, he positioned himself between her and the brood mares, blocking their escape. Once she and the pony were on the other side, he swung the gate shut.

"Thank you," she said when he turned around.

"Good thing I happened by. You'd have had a stampede to contend with."

"My hero." Her teasing tone matched the twinkle in her eyes.

"Let me remove that too-small shoe, and I'll really be your hero."

"What about your meeting with Mercer?"

"It can wait."

A small exaggeration. Ryder's father had little patience with people who kept him waiting. Even so, Ryder didn't change his mind.

They began a slow, painful procession toward the barn. If possible, Ryder would have carried the pony. Fortunately, before long, they reached an empty stall.

"I'll get a rasp and a pair of hoof clippers."

"I'll show you where they're kept."

"Not necessary."

The curiosity was back in her eyes. "I suppose you know where the tack room is, too."

"Center aisle."

"You have been here before."

Feeling her stare following him, he grinned and strode down the aisle toward the tack room. The next instant, he remembered his hard-learned lesson and sobered.

Voluntarily resigned. In order to join his family's business.

That was what his letter to Madison-Monroe Concepts had cited, though there was nothing voluntary about Ryder's termination. He'd quit his job as senior marketing executive rather than be involved in a messy lawsuit with him named as the defendant. At his lawyer's suggestion, he'd left Phoenix the second the ink was dry on the settlement agreement and before his former boss changed his mind.

Which, technically, made him four days early, not late to his meeting with his father.

No one in his family knew the details of his termination. As far as they were concerned, Ryder had undergone a change of heart, prompted by his father's insistence the

Easy Money needed a top-notch marketing expert to guide their rapidly growing bucking stock business and a wish to better know his much younger sister, Liberty.

There it was again, *massaging* the truth to obtain a positive slant. In this case, Ryder had his reasons.

By the time he returned to the stall, the woman had tied the pony to a metal pole by the door. Ryder removed his suit jacket and draped it over the stall wall. He'd been warm anyway. September in Arizona was a lot like summer in other states. Next, he unbuttoned the cuffs on his dress shirt and rolled up the sleeves.

The woman—should he introduce himself in order to learn her name?—worriedly combed her fingers through the pony's long mane. "Are you sure we shouldn't call the vet first? My kids will be devastated if anything happened to Cupcake."

So, he'd been right. She did have children. Which meant there was a father somewhere in the picture. Ryder was almost relieved and promptly dialed down the charm.

"She'll be fine. I promise."

Lifting the pony's sore hoof, he balanced it on his bent knee. Next, he removed the rasp from his back pocket where he'd placed it and began filing down the ends of the nails used to fasten the shoe to the hoof. Once that was done, the shoe could be removed without causing further damage to the hoof. A few good pries with the clippers, and the shoe fell to the stall floor with a dull clink.

Ryder gently released Cupcake's hoof and straightened. He swore the pony let out an audible sigh.

"She'll feel brand-new by morning."

"You won't take offense if I have Mercer look at her?" the woman said. "Just to be on the safe side."

"Not at all." Ryder chuckled. "I wouldn't trust me, either, if I were you." He brushed at his soiled slacks. "Given the clothes."

She flashed him that gorgeous smile.

Kids. Likely a husband. He had to remember that. She'd be an easy one to fall for, and Ryder had a bad habit of choosing unwisely. Just look at his current situation. Unemployed and returning home all because he'd gotten involved with the wrong person.

"By the way, I'm—"

"Hey, there you are!" Ryder's father walked briskly toward them, his whiskered face alight with joy. "I've been waiting."

"Sorry. Got waylaid." All the tension that had seeped out earlier returned. New knots formed. Sooner or later, he was going to have to tell his father the truth about the real reason he'd quit his job, and he wasn't looking forward to it. "How are you, Dad?" Outside the stall, the two men engaged in a back-thumping hug.

"Good, now that you're here." He held Ryder at arm's length. "Glad to see you, son."

"I was helping…" Ryder turned to the woman, a little taken aback by her startled expression.

"You're Ryder Beckett?" The question hinged on an accusation.

"On my good days."

Only his father laughed. "You should hear what they call him on his bad days."

The woman stared at him. "You weren't supposed to be here till Saturday."

"I got away early." Ryder felt his defenses rising, though he wasn't sure why. And how was it she knew his schedule? That elusive familiarity from earlier returned. "Have we met before?"

"This is Tatum Mayweather," his father said. "You remember her. She's your sister Cassidy's best friend."

Tatum. Of course. The name brought his vague memories into sharp focus. "It's been a lot of years," he said by way of an excuse.

"It has." She removed the halter from Cupcake and shut

the stall door behind her. "If you'll excuse me, my lunch hour is over, and I need to get back to work. Your mother's been answering the phone for me in the house."

"Guess I'll see you around, then."

"Sure."

"Bright and early tomorrow morning." His father beamed. "Tatum's our office manager. After I give you a tour of the bucking stock operation, she can go over our contracts with you."

Office manager. That explained her cool reaction to him.

If Ryder accepted his family offer to be the arena's new head of marketing and client relations, he'd be in charge of advertising and promotion, duties currently performed by Tatum.

"Look, it's not…"

What could he say? That he wasn't after her job? Okay, maybe he was, but only parts of it and only temporarily. She, however, didn't know that.

"See you in the morning." She left, her movements no longer graceful but stilted.

Well, at least Ryder didn't have to worry about becoming involved with a coworker. Any chance of that happening was walking away with Ms. Mayweather.

Only after she'd disappeared through a door across from the tack room did Ryder realize she hadn't asked Mercer to check on Cupcake.

RYDER'S FATHER KEPT up a near constant stream of conversation as they covered the short distance from the barn to the house. "Thanks for coming. It means a lot to me. Your mother, too."

It was no secret Ryder's father still loved his ex-wife and intended to win her back. Ryder had agreed to help and support him with the expansion of the rodeo arena. He didn't, however, understand his father's enduring feelings regarding his mother.

"Hope you're hungry," his father said. "Your mother's fixed enough food for a dozen people."

"I don't want her going to any trouble."

"Your early arrival put her in quite a tizzy. She made an emergency run to the grocery store last night just to have the food you like on hand."

"I'm not picky, Dad."

"Well, this is a big day for her. She's nervous."

She wasn't the only one. Ryder had been fighting anxiety for days now.

Five years was a long time to go without seeing one's mother. They'd spoken on the phone, but only occasionally when he happened to call his sisters. Mostly on birthdays and Christmas. One or the other insisted he talk to their mother, too. He usually relented, solely for his sisters' sakes. Ryder simply couldn't get past what he saw as his mother's betrayal.

His father always defended his mother, saying she was right to divorce him. Ryder didn't see it that way. She cared only about herself and hadn't once considered the effect losing their father would have on her children.

Her selfishness, however, wasn't the only reason his return was difficult. She'd lied. For twenty-five years. To everyone. And like the divorce, the lies had stolen parts of their lives they could never get back.

"The girls can't wait to see you." His father talked about Ryder's grown sisters as if they were young. Then again, Cassidy had been only ten when their parents divorced, to Ryder's twelve, and Liberty not even born yet. His father probably did think of Ryder's sisters as "girls." "Cassidy's volunteering at Benjie's school this morning," he continued, "and Liberty's in Globe, picking up lumber. That young man of hers is coming to lunch, too."

"You like him?"

"If you're asking me, is he good enough for her, the answer is yes. I like him. Hell, I fixed 'em up."

"That's not the story I heard. You darn near ruined their relationship."

"Water under the bridge."

Ryder's sister obviously possessed a forgiving heart. "What's the lumber for? Fences?"

"Building jumps. We teach English hunter classes now, if you can believe that. Part of our outreach program with the school. We offer riding instruction to students for a discount price. Your mother's on the school board and spearheaded the whole thing."

"I had no idea." What else would Ryder learn about his mother during his stay? Did he care?

"It's good for the arena, and it's good for the community. Gives the students something to do in the afternoons and on weekends. Reckless is a small town without funding for local sports programs. But you know that as well as anyone."

Ryder did. He'd grown up in Reckless until he was fourteen and legally old enough to choose which of his parents he wanted to live with. On the day after his birthday, he'd packed his suitcase. A week later, when nothing his mother said or did and no amount of tears she cried made a difference, Ryder boarded a bus to Kingman where his father had moved.

For a few weeks each summer, he came back. That ended once Ryder graduated high school and left for college, allowing the rift between him and his mother to widen.

Then, a few months ago, Liberty discovered she shared the same biological father as her siblings and made contact, inviting him to Reckless for the purpose of getting acquainted. He did that, along with exercising his right to half ownership of the arena. When Ryder's mother objected, he threatened her with legal action. Having little choice, she eventually caved.

The result, the Becketts were now all in one place, though not reunited. Perhaps that was too much to ask.

His father led Ryder through the spacious backyard with its well-tended lawn. The swings and slide from Ryder's youth were gone, replaced by one of those multicolored modular play sets, he assumed for his nephew, Benjie. Just as well. Ryder sported a three-inch scar on his forearm, proof that the swings and slide had been old and dilapidated even in his day.

His father opened the kitchen door without knocking and called, "Sunny, you here?"

Though his father didn't live at the arena—he rented a small place in town—Ryder suspected he was a frequent visitor to the house. Apparently his mother really was softening toward him.

Her response drifted to them from down the hall. "Be right out."

Ryder paused inside the door.

"Don't just stand there." His father beckoned him with a wave. "It's not like you're a stranger."

Wrong. Ryder was a stranger. He'd lived many more years in Phoenix than Reckless—a mere seventy miles away, yet it might as well have been a million.

He advanced three whole feet before coming to another halt. That was all the distance required to walk from the present straight into the past, and the sensation knocked him off-kilter.

While he stood there, his father went to the fridge and helped himself to a chilled bottled water, further confirming Ryder's suspicions that he was a regular visitor.

"You want one?" He held out a second bottle.

"Thanks." Funny how Ryder's throat had gone completely dry. He accepted the bottle, twisted off the cap and took a long swallow. The cold water restored his balance.

Footsteps warned him of his mother's approach. He had but a few seconds to replace the bottle cap and prepare himself before she appeared.

"Ryder!" Cheeks flushed, she hurried toward him.

He tried to form his mouth into something resembling a smile. He must have succeeded, for she beamed.

"I'm so happy you came."

"It's good to see you, Mom." He uttered the words automatically.

They hugged, his mother clinging to him while Ryder gave her shoulders a perfunctory squeeze. He'd accepted his father and Liberty's invitation, it was his responsibility to deal with the consequences. Beside them, his father grunted with approval.

"Are you hungry?" His mother released him and brushed self-consciously at her hair, which was styled perfectly and in no need of tidying. "I made chili and corn bread."

His favorite meal as a boy. All right, it was still one of his favorite meals. Maybe because it reminded him of the good times, before their lives had imploded.

"Great. Thanks."

After an awkward moment of silence, she said, "I see you got a water."

"I did."

She skimmed her palms down the sides of her jeans. "We could sit in the living room. If you want. Until your sisters get here. Or outside. Though it's hot."

"Anywhere's fine with me," Ryder said. He'd be on edge and defensive regardless of his surroundings.

His father must have taken pity on his mother, for he said, "Let's sit at the kitchen table. Like the old days."

Ryder wasn't sure about the old days, but he reached for a chair. The same one he'd sat in as a child.

Abruptly, he moved his hand to the next chair over. He refused to slip into former habits just because he was back in Reckless, even habits as seemingly harmless as which chair he occupied.

An awkward silence descended. For no reason really, Ryder attempted to fill it with small talk. "How have you been, Mom?"

"All right. Busy. We now have weekly team penning competitions and bull-riding jackpots, monthly roping clinics and have almost doubled the number of riding classes offered. The Wild West Days Rodeo is in a couple of weeks."

As a kid, Ryder had loved Wild West Days. The week-long, town-wide event included a parade, an outdoor arts-and-crafts festival, food vendors, square dancing and mock gunfights. Cowfolk and tourists alike traveled halfway across the country to participate in both the rodeo at the Easy Money and the other activities.

Ryder's mind went in the direction it always did. "Have you done any promotion?"

"The usual," his mother answered.

"Which is?"

"Tatum updated the website a couple months ago. We've sent out notices, both email and postcards. There are posters and flyers in town."

In Ryder's opinion, posters and flyers in town were a complete waste of resources. There was no need to advertise locally. The goal was to bring outsiders to Reckless.

"Have you considered reciprocating with other rodeo arenas?" he asked.

"What do you mean?"

"Ask them to advertise our rodeo in exchange for advertising theirs."

"Why would our competition do us any favors?" his father asked. "Or us them?" The question wasn't intended to criticize. He appeared genuinely interested.

"It's not competition as long as the rodeos fall in different months."

"Would they go along? The other arenas?"

"We can ask."

His parents exchanged glances, then his father shrugged. "I say yes."

"I think it's a great idea."

To Ryder's ears, his mother's enthusiasm rang false. He wanted to tell her that she didn't need to endorse his ideas just because she was glad to have him home.

"Tatum can compile a list of potential rodeo arenas in the morning," his father suggested.

His mother readily agreed. "I'll ask her."

"Or Ryder can. They're already meeting."

Yeah. Ryder couldn't help wondering how that would go.

The back door abruptly swung open, and his sister Liberty burst into the kitchen, followed closely by a tall cowboy. Ryder guessed the man to be his future brother-in-law.

He'd barely stood when she threw herself at him. "Ryder!"

Unlike with his mother, the hug he gave his baby sister was filled with affection. "Hey, pip-squeak. How are you?"

She buried her face in the front of his shirt. "Better now."

He leaned back to look at her. "You're not crying, are you?"

"Absolutely not." She sniffed and wiped at her nose.

Ryder pulled her close again, his heart aching. Not spending time with Liberty, not getting to watch her grow up, was one of his biggest regrets about leaving Reckless and his main reason for returning. That, and guilt. She'd suffered the most from their mother's lies. If he could make up for that in some small way, he would.

"I'm really happy you came."

Would she say that, love him less, if she knew the other reason for his return?

"After a week, you'll probably be sick of me," he said.

"Not going to happen." Liberty turned to her fiancé. "This is Deacon."

Ryder wasn't the sentimental sort, but the tender way she spoke Deacon's name affected him. He was glad she'd found happiness; she certainly deserved it.

What kind of mother lied to her child about the identity

of her father? The same one who thought only of herself and not her children when she unceremoniously tossed their father out and refused to let him back into their lives.

"Nice to finally meet you." Putting thoughts of his mother aside, Ryder shook Deacon's hand. "I've heard good things about you."

"Same here."

In his line of work, Ryder often made snap judgments. Deacon's handshake was firm and offered without hesitation. A good sign. Ryder decided he approved of his sister's choice in husband.

The pleasantries that followed were cut short when Cassidy and, to Ryder's surprise, Tatum Mayweather arrived to join them. Wasn't she supposed to be at work?

For a moment, he and Cassidy simply stared at each other. Once, they'd been inseparable. Then, their parents divorced, and sides were declared. Ryder had chosen their father's, Cassidy their mother's. Growing apart from her was another of his regrets.

He made the first move and opened his arms. She stepped into his embrace, and Ryder swore everyone in the room visibly relaxed.

The hug ended too soon. "Mom," Cassidy said, "I hope you don't mind, I asked Tatum to lunch. She didn't get a chance to eat. Too busy taking care of Cupcake."

"Of course not."

Tatum smiled apologetically. "I hate imposing on your reunion."

"Nonsense. You're like family."

For someone considered to be like family, Tatum looked ready to bolt. Ryder found that interesting. Then again, he found a lot of things about her interesting. Good thing that, as a Beckett employee, she was off-limits.

With everyone pitching in, lunch was soon on the table. Liberty had inherited their father's conversational abilities, and between the two of them, there were no more lulls.

That was, until Cassidy said, "Tatum mentioned you two didn't recognize each other."

"It's true," Ryder admitted.

Tatum echoed his earlier remark. "It's been a while. We've both changed."

"Do you forget all the women you kiss?" Cassidy asked, a teasing lilt to her voice. "Or just the first one?"

"Kiss?" He had forgotten.

In a rush, it all came back to him. The Valentine's Day card. Tatum's desperate look of hope. The casual peck on the cheek he'd given her.

"I'd have bet money you wouldn't remember," Cassidy said.

An undefinable emotion filled Tatum's eyes before she averted her glance. Something told Ryder this had been some sort of test and that he'd failed it.

Chapter Two

It took a full five minutes for Tatum's cheeks to cool. How could Cassidy embarrass her like that? They were best friends. Lifelong best friends.

Worse than embarrassing her, Cassidy had intentionally used that long ago chaste kiss—Tatum had been just twelve and Ryder nearly fourteen—to deliver a dig to her brother. Tatum neither wanted to nor deserved to be dragged into any feud between the siblings.

And, seriously, wasn't it past time they let bygones be bygones? Mercer was sober. He and Sunny were working together running the arena and getting along. For the most part. Business was booming. Liberty had forgiven her mother's duplicity and was making up for lost years with Mercer by spending time with him. Ryder had come home. Cassidy alone refused to let go of the past.

Tatum's anger continued to simmer all during the lunch. Cassidy should be glad her brother had returned. For her mother's sake, if nothing else. Sunny had hated losing Ryder and longed for a reconciliation with him since the day he left to live with Mercer. As a mother herself, Tatum sympathized. She'd been separated only briefly from her children this past spring, yet it had been the worst four months of her life.

Cassidy was also a mother, though Benjie's father had never been in the picture. Ever. She didn't have to share her child with an ex or contend with a former, impossible to please, mother-in-law. Tatum sighed. Lucky Cassidy.

"Dad, maybe after lunch you can take a look at Tatum's pony."

Her head shot up at hearing Ryder speak her name.

"What's wrong with Cupcake?" Mercer asked, shoveling a large bite of chili into his mouth.

Tatum swallowed before answering. "I, um, thought she might have foundered. Ryder says her limp's due to a poorly fitted shoe."

"One way to find out is remove the shoe."

"He…already did that." What was wrong with her? She couldn't string a simple sentence together without tripping over her words.

Her glance strayed to Ryder, the cause of her unease, though, why, she had no idea. He meant nothing to her, outside of being the recipient of her one-sided childhood crush. The kiss—peck, she corrected herself—while important to her, had meant little to him. She'd presented him with a homemade Valentine's Day card that she'd labored over for days. He read it, then dipped his head and brushed her cheek with his lips. The next week, he'd left to live with Mercer in Kingman, dashing her fragile hopes and dreams.

Over the years, the memory of her first crush changed, from painful to one she viewed with mild amusement and even fondness. Too bad Cassidy had to go and tarnish that for her.

"Is the foot warm?" Mercer asked, still talking about Cupcake.

"No," Ryder replied before Tatum could.

Not that she'd have known if the foot was warm or not. She hadn't checked. Running into Ryder had distracted her.

"Then she probably isn't foundered." Mercer scraped the last of the chili from his bowl. "Ryder has a good eye when it comes to horses."

"I'm sure she'll be fine." Tatum wished the conversation would shift from her to something else. Like Liberty and Deacon's upcoming wedding.

"Where is she?"

"Cupcake? I moved her to the horse barn. In that empty stall next to the gray Percheron."

"I'll take a look at feeding time." Mercer patted his stomach as if to settle his meal.

Tatum felt Ryder's gaze on her and struggled to ignore him. It was impossible. The green-gray color of his eyes was unlike any she'd seen, made more prominent by his strong, masculine features and short cropped brown hair.

To her chagrin, her heart gave a little flutter in return. Good grief. Surely she couldn't be attracted to him. He wasn't her type. More than that, he could well be after her job.

Hoping to hide her reaction, she said, "Thank you, Mercer. From me and my kids. You know how they love Cupcake."

"How old are they?" Ryder's mouth curved at the corners into a devastatingly charming smile.

Tatum responded by blushing. And all because Cassidy had made Tatum acutely aware of Ryder by mentioning that stupid kiss. When they finished with lunch she was going to give her best friend a well-deserved piece of her mind.

"My daughter's seven, and the boys are four and two."

"Are they in school with Benjie?"

"My daughter is, though not in the same grade. The boys attend day care while I work."

It had been difficult finding reliable and reasonably priced child care in such a small town. The Becketts paid Tatum a fair, even generous, wage. Still, a large chunk of her income went to cover the costs of day care. And rent and food. Making ends meet was a delicate balance. Luckily, her ex paid his child support on time and carried the children as dependents on his health insurance.

If for any reason, that ceased, Tatum would be back to where she was earlier this year. Unable to provide her children with the most basic necessities and at risk of losing them.

The Becketts hadn't just given her a job when Tatum was laid off, they'd saved her family. Her loyalty to them was deep and abiding.

"Tatum's a teacher," Liberty said.

"Was," Tatum corrected.

"You teach art classes."

"Really?" Ryder looked at her with interest.

"Just part-time. Lenny Faust at the Ship-With-Ease Store lets me use the empty space next door. I used to teach third and fourth grade at the elementary school. For seven years." Why had she felt pressured to qualify herself? As if teaching art wasn't good enough.

"Until last December," Cassidy added with disgust. "That's when the school board gave her the boot. Bad decision."

"Now, now," Sunny admonished. "We've been over this before. There are other teachers who've been with the school longer."

"Budget cuts. Right. You were outvoted, and your hands are tied."

"We'll hire Tatum back as soon as we can." Sunny covered the leftover corn bread with a linen napkin. "The board convenes in a few weeks to approve the new budget."

Tatum didn't want to get her hopes up, but she couldn't help herself. She loved teaching. Other than her own children, nothing gave her greater satisfaction or enjoyment, and she missed it terribly.

To her vast relief, talk turned to the upcoming Wild West Days Rodeo and the arena's record number of entries.

"Ryder has some notion about...what did you call it?"

"Reciprocal advertising," Ryder said, then went on to explain the concept.

Tatum thought the idea innovative, though her experience with marketing was limited to her job at the arena and what Sunny had taught her.

Cassidy shrugged. "We've always done well enough without having to swap advertising with other rodeo arenas."

"We could do better," Ryder said.

"What if it backfires and we lose business?"

"Nothing ventured, nothing gained. Look at what Dad's done with the bulls he purchased. He told me revenue's increased over fifteen percent in two months."

"Because of the weekly bull-riding jackpots and team penning."

"It's just an idea, Cassidy. I'm not married to it."

Ryder's response was casual, as if he couldn't care less. A stillness of his hand and tension in his jaw gave Tatum the impression he cared very much and didn't like his methods being questioned.

The Beckett family dynamics were certainly interesting and, at times, bewildering and frustrating. Did none of them realize this was the first time in who knew how many years they were all together? Couldn't they play nice this once?

Excusing herself, Tatum said, "Duty calls. My voicemail box has probably reached its limit and is ready to self-destruct."

"And I have a meeting with a client." Deacon pushed back from the table. "Thank you for lunch, Sunny."

"I'll walk you to your truck." Before joining Deacon, Liberty bent and gave Ryder a quick kiss on the cheek. "I'm really glad you're home. Let's have dinner soon."

"How about tomorrow night? I need someone to show me around town. A lot's changed."

"Great! Deacon and I will pick you up at seven."

A smile spread across Ryder's face, and Tatum was momentarily disarmed by his handsomeness. It was amazing, really, that, at thirty-six, he remained a bachelor. Women no doubt pursued him in droves.

One by one, everyone left the kitchen. Cassidy had to supervise preparations for the roping practice later that afternoon. Once Liberty saw Deacon off, she'd recruit a couple of the wranglers to help her unload the lumber she'd bought. Mercer was taking Ryder to his place to settle in.

Sunny started clearing the table.

Though she'd been the one to suggest leaving, Tatum offered, "I can stay and help, if you want."

"Thanks. Then I'll go with you to the office. There's a pile of paperwork calling my name."

Ryder paused on his way to the door, stopping Tatum as she carted an armload of dishes to the sink. "See you in the morning?"

"Right."

He didn't move. "Look, I'm sorry."

"For what?"

"Not remembering. The kiss." Those compelling eyes roved her face, then lingered on her mouth. "That wouldn't happen now, I guarantee it."

The next instant, he was gone. Thank goodness! One second longer, and he'd have heard her sharp intake of breath.

Tatum tried to tell herself that Ryder was in marketing. Essentially a salesman. Winning people over, even flirting a little, was part of the job and second nature to him. Yet, a thrill wound slowly through her, confirming just how susceptible she was to him. She simultaneously dreaded the coming morning and couldn't wait for it.

CASSIDY SAT AT the front desk when Ryder entered the ranch office. "Hi. Tatum's not here yet."

Her tone wasn't exactly welcoming, but neither was it distant. Did she consider him an interloper rather than an asset to the business? She still treated his father that way at times.

"I came early to see you."

It had been easy enough to learn from his father that Cassidy made a habit of visiting the office ahead of Tatum, who had to drop off her sons at day care. She liked to review the day's schedule and answer emails. According to their father, it was the only break she'd have all day.

"I didn't come empty-handed." He produced two paper cups of steaming coffee. Sitting in the visitor chair across from her, he passed her the cup with caramel latte scrawled in black marker on the side.

After a pause, she accepted it. "Dad tell you this is my favorite?"

"I've been picking his brain."

"You actually stood in line twenty minutes for coffee?" Cassidy sipped tentatively through a hole in the plastic lid.

"I got up early and beat the morning rush. Who'd've guessed? Reckless has a gourmet coffee shop."

She eyed him from over the brim of her cup. "Things change."

He eyed her back. "They do."

"Is this a peace offering or a bribe?"

"I don't want to fight, Cassidy."

She set down the coffee. "We're not fighting."

"You embarrassed Tatum yesterday just to get at me."

"I do owe her an apology."

"If I didn't know better, I'd think you're sorry I came home."

"Why wouldn't I be glad? Really. Mom's ready to burst with happiness. And Liberty's so excited, she's downright annoying. The whole family's reunited at last, yadda, yadda, yadda."

"What about you?"

"Depends."

"On?"

"Mom, for one. You broke her heart when you left. I don't want you to do it again."

"The only promise I made Dad and Liberty when I agreed to come here was that I'd try."

"An honest effort is all I ask."

Did she think he'd give anything less? "Mom and I have a lot of bridges to mend. It won't be easy."

"It's going to be as easy or difficult as you make it."

Interesting comment for someone who was starting out by making things difficult. But, his sister was probably right. "Let's stick to the reason I waited twenty minutes in line for overpriced coffee."

"I thought you said you beat the rush."

"A slight exaggeration."

Cassidy laughed. It wasn't much of a laugh. More like a dry chuckle. Still, it beat the heck out of their mother's forced cheerfulness at lunch the day before.

"Why are you really mad at me?" he asked.

"Tatum. She needs this job, Ryder. And you're a threat to it."

"Not as much as you think."

"Dad has other ideas."

Ryder considered leveling with Cassidy about this being a temporary stay until he landed another position. Gut instinct made him hesitate. "I'm not a threat to Tatum."

"When she lost her job at the school, she also lost custody of her kids."

"Wow! You're kidding."

"Temporarily lost custody. But she fell apart."

"What happened?"

"Tatum's good with money. But the divorce left her without any kind of nest egg. And you know what teachers make, especially in Reckless. Squat. She had no savings to fall back on when the school board laid her off last December. The extra money she makes off of her art classes is barely enough to put groceries on the table."

"Couldn't she find another teaching job outside of Reckless?"

"That takes time. She also had her house to consider. She didn't want to move if she could help it."

If anyone understood the difficulty of finding a good job and dwindling resources, it was Ryder. The past two months of searching had produced no results other than draining his bank account. Though what hindered his job search had less to do with lack of available employment and more to do with the bad reputation he'd created for himself at Madison-Monroe Concepts.

His stomach involuntarily tightened. He'd live down his mistake. Eventually. Come hell or high water.

"We gave her a job as office manager," Cassidy continued, "and that took a lot of arm-twisting. Tatum is proud and refused what she called a pity job."

"Dad says she's pretty good at what she does."

"She is. Which is why it's not a pity job. But then the bank foreclosed on her house anyway when she couldn't keep up with the payments. She and the kids moved in with us. Rent free. That *was* charity, and she struggled to accept it."

"Seven people. Four bedrooms. It must have been crowded."

"We didn't care. But her ex-mother-in-law got wind of the situation and convinced her son to hire an attorney, claiming Tatum couldn't provide adequately for the kids."

"He sued for custody?" Ryder was appalled. "Why didn't he help her make her mortgage payments? They're his children, too."

"It didn't go that far. Luckily. Tatum compromised. She turned over care of the kids to her mother-in-law. Just until she saved enough money working for us to rent an apartment. It was a rough period for her. The kids, too. They missed Tatum and hated living with their grandmother."

"Did she mistreat them?"

"No, no. She's not the warm, cookie-baking kind of grandmother, but that wasn't the problem. She lives in Glendale. A four-hour round trip. Tatum only saw the kids once a week at most. The day she signed the lease on her apartment, she broke down and cried in front of the rental agent."

"She's lucky to have you and Mom."

"We're lucky to have her. She works hard, even if an office manager isn't her first choice of a job."

"I do remember her drawing a lot. Always walking around with a sketchbook."

Cassidy studied him critically. "So, you didn't forget her entirely."

"No." But he hadn't thought of her in years. A stark contrast to the past twenty-four hours. She'd been on his mind constantly. "You and she barrel raced."

"We did. She met her ex on the circuit, and for a few years, they traveled from rodeo to rodeo, living in an RV. That wore thin on Tatum. She quit in order to obtain her teaching degree."

"Her husband continued to compete?"

"Nothing would stop him. Tatum did her best to make the marriage work. Full-time job, full-time mom, part-time husband. When she got pregnant for the third time, he left for good, saying something like, 'baby, I just can't be tied down.' She took it hard. I say the jerk didn't deserve her, and she was better off without him."

Ryder tended to agree.

"I'm not gossiping, so don't think that." Cassidy sipped again at her coffee. "I only wanted you to know what Tatum's been through and why this job is important to her." Her voice dropped. "Don't mess it up for her."

"I won't. I promise."

Cassidy looked skeptical.

"My plan is to create and implement a sound marketing strategy for the arena." One Tatum or his mother could manage after he was gone.

Funny. He hadn't realized until this moment how similar his and Tatum's situations were. Both of them working interim jobs while hoping for a better one. Both of them resisting to take what they considered charity.

Okay, maybe that wasn't so funny.

"What exactly is going on with Mom and Dad?" Ryder didn't want to talk about Tatum anymore. "Do you think they'll get back together?"

"God, I hope not." Cassidy turned away from him to stare out the window.

It wasn't eight in the morning, yet the ranch was alive with activity. Hands cleaning stalls. Customers exercising their horses. The carpenters Liberty had hired to construct the horse jumps were making a ruckus behind the barn, banging hammers and running the chain saw. Mercer conferred with a rep from the grain dealer.

"For once I agree with you."

Her head swung back around. "Why do I think there's a catch?"

"No catch. Mom threw him out. Abandoned him in his hour of need. Lied to him about being Liberty's father. He'd be a fool to get involved again."

"She had every right to throw him out," Cassidy argued hotly. "He's an alcoholic."

Their parents had purchased the Easy Money before Ryder was born and had taken it from a run-down, dirt-poor arena to the best facility in the southern part of the state. That all changed when Ryder's grandfather died suddenly from a heart attack, and his father began drowning his grief with whiskey. Daily.

In less than a year, the arena went from prospering to

the verge of bankruptcy, and Ryder's mother kicked him to the curb. What Ryder knew and his sisters didn't until recently was that their father retained his half ownership of the arena. Their mother had also never paid their father his share of the profits per their settlement agreement. The sum was staggering.

"Reformed alcoholic," Ryder said. "He hasn't touched a drink in over twenty years." He'd stopped shortly after Ryder moved in with him.

"Once an alcoholic, always—"

"Let it go, Cassidy."

"He didn't almost kill you!"

"It was a fender bender. You were fine."

She drew back, her expression one of shock. "What if he'd been going faster?"

One night, their father had picked up Cassidy en route home from the bar. While pulling on to the property, he'd lost control of the truck and rammed into the well house. He'd been sorry. Their mother outraged.

"Mom was justified. He wasn't only a lousy husband, he was a danger to our well-being."

"He's paid for his sins, Cassidy. We all have. Mom divorced him and told everyone some cowboy passing through was Liberty's father. Our little sister deserved to know the truth. Mom had no right denying either her or Dad."

"She had her reasons. Good ones."

"Two wrongs don't make a right."

"In this case, they do."

"She didn't just reject him." Ryder's anger rose, its grip like a vise around his chest. "She tore our family apart. Took our father away from us. That wasn't fair."

"She's not the only one to tear our family apart." Tears welled in Cassidy's eyes.

"What are you saying?"

"You left. And you hardly ever visited. You're only here

now because you quit your job. You don't love us or want us. We're just your last resort."

Ryder sat in stunned silence. She thought *he'd* rejected *them*?

Before he could say more, Tatum entered the office. One glance at them, and she pulled up short. "Sorry. Am I interrupting?"

Chapter Three

Both Ryder and Cassidy insisted that Tatum hadn't inadvertently walked in on a private and sensitive conversation. She didn't believe them. Ryder had stood so fast, he almost upended the visitor chair. Cassidy averted her gaze but not before Tatum spied the look of utter distress on her friend's face.

Old wounds. When the Becketts weren't hiding them, they were poking them with sharp sticks.

"Why don't we start with a tour of the place?" Ryder suggested, depositing his empty coffee cup into the wastebasket near Tatum's desk. That put him in close proximity to Cassidy, and she noticeably tensed. "If you're free," he added.

He must have visited the Dawn to Dusk Coffee shop on his way in this morning. Cassidy wouldn't have gone despite her penchant for caramel lattes. "I shouldn't leave the office unattended," Tatum said. Lunch yesterday had been an exception. Usually Sunny relieved her.

"It's okay," Cassidy volunteered. "I'll watch the phones."

"Are you sure?" Tatum was about to suggest that Cassidy give her brother the tour when he cut her short.

"Come on." He motioned toward the door.

"Let me put my things away first."

"Meet you in the barn." The next instant, he was gone.

Wow. Whatever had happened between him and his sister must have been worse than Tatum thought. She stowed her lunch in the small countertop refrigerator and her purse in the desk drawer.

"You okay?" she asked Cassidy in a whisper, though Ryder was well beyond earshot.

"I'm sorry about yesterday. I shouldn't have mentioned the kiss."

"We were kids." Tatum straightened, her previous anger at her friend dissipating.

"Yeah, but it was a big deal for you. At the time."

"Forget about it, okay?" On impulse, Tatum gave her friend's shoulders a quick squeeze.

"What was that for?"

"Do I need a reason?"

"I guess not." Cassidy's face relaxed. "Go on, get out of here. I need my daily dose of Facebook."

Tatum laughed. It was a joke the two frequently shared. Both were borderline workaholics and wouldn't ever wile away the hours surfing the net.

In the barn, she met up with Ryder. "Where do you want to start?"

"How's Cupcake?"

They strolled the long aisle. "I haven't had a chance to check on her this morning."

"Let's start there."

"She's better," Tatum had to admit after they took the pony on a short walk around the wash bays.

"When's the farrier due next?"

"Unless there's an emergency, he's here every Thursday."

"She'll be okay until then. If you do take her out for a ride, put a hoof boot on her."

"Thank you. I probably shouldn't have doubted you."

"It was the clothes." He smiled.

Tatum had to stop herself from ogling. Today he wore jeans, a Western-cut shirt that molded nicely to his broad shoulders and a cowboy hat that was scuffed in all the right places. He looked as if he'd never left the ranch.

"What made you give up rodeoing?" She recalled Sunny bragging on her son, who'd won several junior rodeo championships before abandoning a promising pro career.

"College."

"Not enough time to do both?"

"Not enough money. Finances were tight. I had to make a choice."

Tatum was familiar with that dilemma. She lived it on a daily basis.

They returned Cupcake to her stall, hung the halter on a nearby peg and continued their tour of the grounds. He was careful to take her arm when they walked over a hole or navigated an obstacle. Tatum didn't need the assistance. She liked it, nonetheless.

"I always figured I'd wind up like my dad and make rodeo my life," he said.

"You're more like your mother than you realize. She's really savvy when it comes to business."

Lines appeared on Ryder's brow. "I hadn't thought of that before."

"It's not a bad thing."

He avoided commenting by asking, "Besides the bulls, what else is new?"

"Not much. Tom Pratt gives monthly roping clinics."

They wandered toward the bull pens, which were located on the other side of the arena, far from the horses. The two didn't always mix, and it was best to maintain a healthy distance between them.

"He was smart to do that. Nothing will grow the arena faster than good bucking stock."

"We can hardly keep up with the requests."

In addition to providing bucking stock for their four annual rodeos, the Easy Money leased horses and now bulls to other rodeos. It was their single highest source of revenue. Tatum had felt guilty when the Becketts first hired her, thinking they were giving her a job solely because she was a close family friend. That opinion soon changed. With the increase in business, she was earning her keep and then some.

What more could Ryder do to grow the business than Mercer already had? It seemed to Tatum they were at their capacity for bucking stock contracts. Unless the Becketts purchased more bulls. Or Ryder assumed even more of Tatum's duties. Then she really would be a charity case.

A pair of lone riders were making use of the arena. Tatum and Ryder stopped at the fence to observe them.

"Dad mentioned the after-school program," he said.

"That's going well. So well, your dad's considering building a second practice ring just for the students."

"But rodeo events are where the real money is."

"Lessons and horse boarding more than pay for themselves."

"I wasn't insinuating Mom and my sisters' contribution weren't an important part of the arena. There's room for both."

As they started for the office, Liberty passed them, riding one horse and leading a second. She stopped to say good morning and to remind Ryder of their dinner plans that evening.

"What are you up to?" Ryder asked her.

"Endurance training. This is a client's horse." She indicated the tall gelding behind her prancing nervously in place. Pulling on the lead rope, she groaned in frustration. "He's raring to go. I'll catch up with you later."

Ryder stared after her. "I wouldn't have guessed she'd be the one to take after Dad. Then again, none of us knew she was related to him."

Tatum and Cassidy had shared many a long discussion about her parents. Tatum understood Sunny's motives for lying to Liberty—she didn't want to give a raging alco-

holic any reason to remain part of their lives. But Tatum
wasn't sure she'd do the same thing in Sunny's shoes, if
only because of the wedge it had driven between Sunny
and Ryder. Losing her children for a mere four months had
been unbearable. Sunny lost Ryder for twenty-two years,
and she still didn't have him back.

"Ready?" she asked.

"Where to now?"

"The outdoor stalls and back pastures," she suggested.

They went in the same direction as Liberty. Ryder,
Tatum noticed, slowed his steps to keep pace with her
shorter strides. He was tall. Her chin barely reached his
shoulder. He must have grown six inches after he left. If
he kissed her now, he'd have to dip his head considerably
further.

Stop it!

The mental reprimand was useless. How could she not
think of Ryder when he walked beside her, near enough
to touch if she extended her hand a mere three inches to
the right?

What had they been talking about? Oh, yeah, lessons
and boarding.

"Liberty's also in charge of the trail rides," Tatum said.
"There's usually one every weekend when we don't have
a rodeo."

"Just one?"

"We don't have enough requests for more than that on
weekends."

"Are they profitable?"

"Actually, yes."

"What's the margin?"

"I'd say about the same as riding lessons."

"How do we advertise the rides? And don't tell me on
the website and posters in town."

"Okay, I won't. But that's what we do."

He muttered under his breath.

"There are tourists in town," she protested. "They see the posters."

"What about the marina at Roosevelt Lake? Do we have a poster in their window?"

"No."

"We should."

Did he notice he was talking in the plural? "Is that more of your reciprocal advertising?"

"You catch on fast."

"I'll call them and ask if we can deliver a poster."

"I'll do it. In fact, I'll just take one over this afternoon. That way, I can bring back one of theirs."

"Good idea." She supposed a face-to-face meeting was better than a phone call. Harder to say no.

Twenty minutes later they were through with the tour. Approaching the office from the outside entrance rather than the barn, they climbed the three steps to the awning-covered porch. Cassidy still sat at Tatum's desk. Sunny wasn't there. Tatum could see her empty office through the open connecting door.

Was she avoiding Ryder? Had Cassidy told her mother about her fight, or whatever it was, with Ryder?

"You're back." Cassidy quickly closed the webpage she had open on the computer and stood.

"Stay longer if you aren't done," Tatum offered.

"It's all right. I have to make a run into Globe for supplies."

"Didn't Liberty do that yesterday?" Ryder asked.

"She bought lumber. I'm getting vet supplies. Dewormer and penicillin. There's been three cases of strangles reported this month in the Mesa area. We don't want to be caught with a low supply if it should move to Reckless."

"That's serious."

Tatum concurred. She'd seen a strangles epidemic before. The highly contagious infection attacked the lymph nodes between a horse's jaw or in its throat and caused flu-like symptoms lasting weeks, if not months. Should the Becketts' bucking stock or boarded horses succumb, their entire business would be in jeopardy.

"It is serious," Cassidy said. "So, if you'll excuse me."

"We can order penicillin online, and for a lot cheaper, with a prescription."

"I've already thought of that." Cassidy lifted her chin. "Doctor Spence is coming tomorrow."

Ryder softened his voice. "I wasn't questioning your abilities."

"See you later."

"That went well," he said after Cassidy left.

Tatum ignored him and sat at her desk.

"Did I say something wrong?"

"Look." She leveled her stare at him. "If you weren't questioning her abilities, you were questioning something."

"You're right." He dropped down into the visitor chair. "I'm sorry to involve you in our squabble."

"Squabble?" That hardly described their longstanding clash.

"This big reconciliation Liberty and Dad are hoping for may not happen."

"It definitely won't happen if you don't try and get along."

"We argued about Mom. And," he admitted, "the way I've acted in recent years."

Big surprise. Not. "How about we institute a new rule? No discussion regarding family at work, unless it relates to work. I'll tell Cassidy and Sunny. You tell Liberty and Mercer." She felt as if she was refereeing a fight between her children.

He considered for a moment, then relented with a shrug. "All right."

"That's what I like to see. Progress." She rolled her chair over to the lateral file cabinet by her desk, deciding they should start the office part of Ryder's orientation with the current bucking stock contracts. She opened the drawer and removed a dozen manila folders. "I probably shouldn't point this out…"

"But you will."

"Your resentment toward your mother. It mirrors Cassidy's toward your father."

"Are you saying we'll never find a common ground?"

"I'm saying there's more common ground than you think." She slapped the folders on to the desk, the impact making a loud noise. "Let's start on these."

RYDER STOPPED TO refuel his truck on the way into Reckless. Based on the number of things he'd accomplished, it had been a productive day. He'd spent the morning with Tatum, interfering with her work but also gaining an understanding of how the office ran, including an overview of the accounting system and record keeping. He and his father had had lunch at the Flat Iron Restaurant with one of the arena's oldest clients.

After that, Ryder had headed to the marina at Roosevelt Lake, posters and flyers on the seat beside him. The marina manager, a crusty old guy who could have played an extra in a *Pirates of the Caribbean* movie, was agreeable to Ryder's suggestion that they help each other out.

On impulse, he'd driven to the outskirts of Globe and the mining company offices. After being passed from one person to the next, he'd finally been granted a meeting with the personnel manager's secretary. The middle-aged woman had listened patiently to his pitch—the Easy Money Rodeo Arena would be a great place for employee parties or retreats. She'd agreed to give the material Ryder left with her to her boss and thanked him for his time.

Productive day. No question about it. But nothing a trained monkey couldn't do. Ryder had been a senior marketing executive in charge of several multimillion-dollar accounts. And here he was, delivering posters and flyers and trolling for business. Something he could have done in high school.

Running errands. Sleeping on the trundle bed in his dad's spare room. Fighting with his sister. He might as well be in high school again.

"Ryder Beckett," someone shouted. "Buddy, is that you?"

He glanced up to see a hefty young man approaching, a friendly grin splitting his full face.

"It is you. Son of a gun!"

"Guilty as charged." Ryder hoped the man's name would come to him without having to ask. "How are you…?" At the last second, his brain kicked in. "Tank."

"Dandy as a pig with slop." They shook hands. "I heard you were back and working for the family."

He'd said *for* the family, not *with* the family. To Ryder, there was a large distinction. Did everyone in town think like Tank, that Ryder had been given a job as opposed to being made a part of the business?

Then again, did he care? He was leaving soon.

Once more, Ryder questioned his motives for returning. He could have chosen somewhere else to lay low. Eventually found temporary employment. But he'd allowed loyalty to his father and Liberty's heartfelt pleas to sway him.

"What happened to that fancy job you had in Phoenix?" Tank asked. "Your mom was always telling everyone what a big shot you were and how much money you made. This must be a step down."

Damned if Tank could hit below the belt.

"Dad asked for my help, and here I am. Family comes first."

"Sure. Course." Tank may or may not have believed Ryder, but he didn't dispute him. "Got me a family of my own now. A wife and little boy."

"Congratulations."

"Heard about your divorce. Sorry, man." Tank didn't sound particularly remorseful or sympathetic.

"It was a long time ago."

Ryder did the math. Thirteen years.

He'd met Sasha, a woman eight years his senior, right out of college, and she was like no one he'd ever known. Confident, sexy and adventurous, in and out of bed. Unfortunately, they fell out of love as quickly as they'd fallen in and spent the next year making each other miserable before coming to their senses.

The only good part about the marriage had been Sasha's little girls. Ryder had liked them and frequently spent more time with them than their own mother did, especially near the end. They, in turn, adored him. Leaving them behind had hurt.

One short-lived relationship after another had him swearing off any commitments for the foreseeable future. This last debacle with his coworker had only reinforced it.

"One of these days, you'll meet the right person," Tank said.

"I guess."

Beside him, the gas nozzle clicked loudly. Ryder reached for it. "Nice seeing you, Tank. You ever bring your family around the Easy Money?"

"We're coming to the Wild West Days Rodeo. Already bought our tickets."

"Good. Looking forward to seeing you there."

They shook hands again, and Ryder climbed into his truck. Starting the engine, he heard Tank's words again— *working for your family*—then slammed the heels of both hands on the steering wheel. He wasn't mad at Tank; he was mad at himself.

Enough was enough. He'd let this happen, he thought, and he could remedy it. Pulling out his smartphone, he went through his saved emails. There! He found it. The one from a friend giving Ryder the name of a headhunter. He dialed the number and set the phone down. The next second, his Bluetooth kicked in, and he could hear ringing through the speaker on his dash. When the receptionist answered, he asked to be put through to Myra Solomon.

"This is Myra."

Ryder introduced himself, giving the name of his friend. "He suggested I give you a call."

"I'm glad you did. Tell me a little about yourself and what kind of job you're looking for."

Ryder talked as he drove, casting his termination in the best possible light. When he finished, Myra groaned tiredly.

"Cut the B.S., Ryder. If we're going to work together, you have to be straight with me. Save the sugarcoated version for prospective employers."

"I quit."

"I know that. I'm interested in why."

"My boss and I didn't share the same visions."

"Whatever happened, we'll work around it," Myra said. "But in order to help you, I have to know what really went down. If not, you're wasting both our time."

Ryder swallowed. He'd been through this before with another headhunter. "I quit rather than be sued."

"For what?"

"Inappropriate conduct."

Myra whistled. "How inappropriate?"

"Not at all."

"Then, why?"

Now it was Ryder's turn to groan. "I was dating a woman at work. One of my subordinates. A member of my team, actually. And before you ask, there was no company policy against employees fraternizing."

"Did you advise HR? Sign any kind of agreement?"

"Yes, we advised HR, and there was no agreement for us to sign. When the relationship ended, I advised HR of that, as well."

"Then, where does the inappropriate conduct come in?"

"We dated for four months. She wanted more, to move in together, and I didn't. Rather than string her along, I ended things."

"That's it?"

"Not entirely. She didn't take the breakup well. She'd call me at all hours and corner me in the office. A couple of our discussions got a little heated. About a week later, one of the other team members received a promotion she was also in line for. She believed I blackballed her."

"And did you?"

"Absolutely not. I was asked for my input on both candidates and gave them both good recommendations. No favoritism. The next day she filed a complaint."

"You just said you showed no favoritism. What were her grounds?"

"During one of those heated discussions, she got carried away. I tried calming her by putting my hand on her arm. She later claimed that I touched her inappropriately."

"Were there any witnesses?"

"A few. They reported seeing me touch her but not where. They weren't close enough."

"Excuse me for stating the obvious, Ryder, but that was stupid. You should have avoided this woman at all costs. Especially after she started calling you. In fact, you should have alerted HR that she was harassing you."

"Live and learn."

"Is any of this in your personnel records?"

"No. That was part of the deal we reached. She dropped the suit, and I quit."

"Well, that's one good thing."

"Not really. Advertising is a small world, and it's filled with big mouths. Even though I did nothing wrong, a lot of companies are reluctant to hire me. She got what she wanted after all."

"Then you move out of state," Myra said matter-of-factly.

"I'm considering it."

"Okay, here's what we're going to do. I'll email you our representation contract. Once you send it back, we'll set up a meeting. Wear your best tie. My assistant will film a short interview with standard questions. We should be able to generate some interest with that. We'll also polish your résumé and rehearse answers to potentially difficult questions. What's your email address?"

They discussed a few more details before disconnecting. Ryder felt both better—he was being proactive and taking steps—and discouraged. How could he have screwed up this badly? Getting involved with a coworker? Worse, a subordinate. He should have his head examined.

Pulling into the arena, he parked by the office and got out. Still plagued by the conversation with the headhunter and not quite ready to face anyone, he went instead to the barn. Without quite realizing where he was going, he found himself standing in front of Cupcake's stall.

The pony snickered and came over for a petting. Ryder automatically gave her a scratch between her short, stubby ears. The next minute, he was in the stall, examining her sore hoof.

"I think you'll live."

Cupcake investigated him, snorting lustily when she encountered his hair.

"Quit it, will you?" Ryder laughed and dropped her hoof.

He and Cassidy once had a pony a lot like this one when they were young. A sorrel named Flame. With two parents involved in rodeo, they'd learned to ride at a very young age.

Suddenly, Ryder missed being on a horse. He'd remedy that this weekend, he decided.

"Hey! What are you doing to our pony?" The annoyed voice belonged to a pint-size girl who, given her long black hair, could only be Tatum's daughter. She stood in the open stall door, hands fisted and planted at her sides.

"Checking her foot."

"I don't know you." The girl backed away and gave Ryder a very suspicious once-over.

"I work here. With your mother."

"Then, why haven't I seen you before?"

"I'm new."

"I'm going to tell my mom."

He expected her to take off running. She didn't. Instead, she opened her mouth and screamed at the top of her lungs.

"Mom!"

"Hey, it's all right. You don't have to—"

She screamed again.

The next second, Tatum came charging up the aisle, one boy in tow, the other, younger one bouncing on her hip. "What's wrong?"

"Nothing," Ryder said.

The girl pointed accusingly at him. "This man is trying to hurt Cupcake."

Chapter Four

"Sorry about that." Tatum suppressed a grin. "I don't know what got into her."

"No harm done. You got here before the police were called."

She walked beside Ryder, carrying her youngest, Adam, because he'd pitched a fit when she tried to put him down. He got that way sometimes after day care, clingy and insecure. The mother in her was patient and understanding of his separation anxiety. The teacher in her wanted him to be more independent. "Gretchen is leery of strangers."

"I noticed."

"She's gotten worse since..." Tatum almost said, since she'd left the kids with her former mother-in-law. Fortunately, she caught herself before having to explain those dark and difficult months. "Lately."

"Who needs a watchdog with Gretchen?"

Tatum took the half smile Ryder offered as an indication he wasn't offended. Not that her daughter had done anything all that awful, other than accuse him of hurting Cupcake. At the top of her lungs.

"She isn't here every day. Cassidy picked up her and Benjie from school, then swung by and got the boys from day care, which is right down the road. We do that a lot. Share driving responsibilities."

"Sounds like a good system."

It was. Two single moms helping each other out. They also swapped turns running errands and babysitting. Not that either of them needed a babysitter much. For dates, at least. Tatum was acutely aware of how a woman in her midthirties with three children, ages seven and under, sent most guys running straight for the hills.

Ryder was among that group. According to Sunny, he was a confirmed, born-again bachelor who put his career first. Not wanting children could be one of his reasons. Or, he might want his own, not a ready-made family.

She'd heard that particular excuse more than once when, last year on a whim, she'd tried internet dating. What a mistake. There was only so much rejection a gal could take.

"How did your visit to the marina go?" she asked.

"We now have a poster in their window." Ryder went on to tell her about his stop at the mining company offices.

She was impressed. No one in the Beckett family had ever reached out to a large corporation before. "If you give me the secretary's name, I'll follow up in a week. Or you can make the call."

"I think that's a good idea. You're probably less pushy than me," he added with a chuckle.

"I was thinking more like she'd listen better to another woman."

His chuckle increased to a laugh. "You've missed your calling, Tatum Mayweather. You'd make a good marketing exec."

"I love my job."

"Which one?"

"Both. Teaching and working here." She did love her job at the ranch, in her way. "Where else can I bring my children with me when we're not busy?"

Gretchen and Drew, her oldest boy, walked ahead of them, Gretchen leading Cupcake and Drew batting stones out of their path with a stick. The pony's limp had completely diminished, and Tatum wasn't worried about letting the children ride her.

To that end, they'd stopped first at the tack room. Rather

than leave, Ryder had insisted on saddling and bridling the pony, though Tatum was more than capable of doing it herself.

"Where to now?"

She pointed at the round pen across from the outdoor stalls. "We usually ride there. Cupcake's small. Less chance of being trampled by bigger, faster-moving horses."

He started ahead.

She had to walk fast in order to keep pace. "Seriously Ryder, I don't want to keep you. I'm sure you have somewhere else to be."

"I've missed working with horses." He opened the gate to the pen and swung it wide.

"A pony ride can't be what you had in mind."

"I'm free until dinner tonight with Liberty and Deacon. Might as well spend the time with you."

Her heart skipped, and, all at once, she was twelve years old again and deep in the throes of a crush. Tatum had grown up with the two older Beckett siblings, she and Cassidy becoming friends in first grade. Funny, Tatum hadn't noticed Ryder much until that last year before he left. She blamed puberty for her heart flutters then. She couldn't say the same thing now.

"Me, first." Drew abandoned his stick the moment they entered the pen.

"My turn. I'm oldest." Gretchen pushed past Drew, grabbing the saddle horn and trying to hoist herself up. She lacked the extra foot in height to manage it on her own.

"Now, now." Tatum set Adam on the ground, but he instantly wrapped his arms around her leg and stuck his thumb in his mouth, a habit he'd mostly given up months ago. Had something happened at day care to prompt this worse-than-usual insecurity? She'd ask in the morning when she dropped him off. "No need to fight. You and Drew can ride Cupcake together."

Their combined weight was easy enough for the sturdy pony to handle.

"I'm not riding with him." If looks could vaporize, Gretchen's younger brother would be no more than a puff of smoke.

"All right," Tatum said evenly. "Then Drew can go first."

"Not fair!" Gretchen shrieked.

Who were these incorrigible monsters? Sure, her children could act up with the best of them. But why today and why in front of Ryder?

"That's enough, young lady. Lower your voice, please."

"But I'm outside."

The argument wasn't entirely illogical. Tatum often chastised her offspring for yelling in the house and cautioned them to "use their inside voices."

"How about you ride Cupcake," Ryder suggested, "and I'll give Drew a piggyback ride?"

Not quite sure she'd heard him right, Tatum stared. She wasn't the only one. Gretchen and Drew did, too, their small mouths slack-jawed.

"You're spoiling them," Tatum insisted.

Without waiting for an answer, Ryder lifted Gretchen on to Cupcake's back and settled her in the saddle. Next, he grabbed Drew by the arms and swung him around on to his back. Drew had to hold tight or he'd have fallen.

Gretchen gave Cupcake a nudge with her heels and jiggled the reins. "Giddyup."

Drew did the same to Ryder, though instead of reins, he tugged on Ryder's shirt collar. Cupcake started out, making a circle of the pen. Ryder followed, with Drew laughing and Gretchen pouting because, in her mind, she'd been trumped by her brother.

"Anyone ever tell you you're a good sport?" Tatum said to Ryder as he passed.

"I need the exercise after driving all day."

Right. If there was an ounce of fat on him, it was buried beneath layers of muscles. The guy was built.

Gripping Adam's hand, she moved to the corner of the pen and watched Ryder play with Drew. The same charm that had won her over yesterday, before she knew who he was, worked its magic on her now. Tatum could hardly catch her breath. Looks and confidence were definitely sexy, but, to her, nothing made a man more attractive than being good with children. Stronger even than a powerful love potion.

During his next pass, his gaze sought hers. Tatum glanced quickly away, afraid her expression would reveal too much.

This beautiful, crazy arrangement lasted five whole minutes. Just long enough for Tatum to fall a little further under his spell. It might have continued longer if Adam didn't suddenly start wailing.

"Wanna ride. Wanna ride."

"Your turn next, sweetie."

"Now!" He let his legs go limp and flung himself to the ground, nearly jerking Tatum's arm from its socket. When she didn't let go, he twisted from side to side. She had ten seconds at most before he succumbed to a complete meltdown. Wouldn't that be icing on the cake?

"Enough, Adam," Tatum said sharply.

In the classroom, be it school or art, and with other people's children, Tatum never lost control or raised her voice. She couldn't make that claim when it came to her own brood, especially when they were testing the limits of her patience like today.

"Ride," Adam howled.

Ryder came over, and Tatum felt her cheeks burn. "Honey, please, stop."

He did. But not because of anything Tatum said or did. Ryder had scooped up the boy and held him close to his chest.

"You really don't have to do this." She wanted to tell Ryder that giving in to Adam's tantrum was teaching him the wrong lesson. She didn't. The boys' giggles were too hard to resist.

"My dad used to cart me and Cassidy around when we were his age."

Tatum had to wonder if her best friend remembered any of the good times with Mercer like her brother obviously did.

"Hey." Gretchen reined Cupcake to a stop in front of them and glared. "Mom says we're not supposed to roughhouse around the horses."

Tatum *did* say that and was frequently ignored. Gretchen likely wanted in on the fun her brothers were having but refused to ask. Next best was ruining their fun.

"It's okay." Drew hugged Ryder's neck harder. "We have an adult present."

Tatum's throat closed. She ached for her children, who missed their father and moments like this. Monty had come around only a few times since their divorce, though his work as an installation foreman for a national auto parts chain brought him to the Phoenix area at least every other month from his home in Flagstaff. Gretchen, old enough and smart enough to figure out that her father didn't want to see her, was especially hurt.

"She's got you there," Tatum told Ryder. "You might spook Cupcake, and Gretchen could fall."

"Aw, no, Mom," Drew threw his head back and wailed.

"Noooo," Adam echoed.

Without missing a beat, Ryder turned toward the gate. "Come on, boys. We've got bigger pastures to ride."

While Gretchen continued circling the pen with Cupcake, an activity that had lost a lot of its appeal, Ryder and the boys frolicked outside the round pen. Before long, Gretchen reached her fill of being excluded and pronounced, "It's Drew's turn."

"Okay." Tatum didn't think either of her sons would abandon Ryder in favor of Cupcake.

Even so, she helped her daughter dismount, then looped Cupcake's reins over a fence railing. "Your turn," Tatum said to Drew upon leaving the pen.

"I don't want to ride."

Of course he didn't. "You need to give Mr. Beckett a rest. He must be tired."

"How about I go with you?" Ryder offered.

Drew bestowed a Christmas-morning smile on him. "All right!"

"Wanna ride," Adam said, refusing to be left out.

"If it's okay with your brother."

"Okay." Drew's joy visibly dimmed. He didn't want to share his new best pal with his brother, but he'd rather share than miss out entirely.

Using one hand, Ryder lifted Drew off his back, then lowered Adam to the ground. He didn't resume sucking his thumb, but he did grab Ryder's leg.

"Daddy!"

Uh-oh. Tatum's stomach dropped to her knees. Could her children not go fifteen minutes without embarrassing her? "Honey, he's not—"

"You stupid dork!" Gretchen shoved her little brother, nearly knocking him over. "He's not our daddy."

"Gretchen! No name-calling. You know better."

Adam burst into sobs. Drew looked ready to cry but held himself in check. Tatum wished for the ground to open up and swallow her and her children whole.

"I'm not your daddy." Ryder lowered himself so that he was eye level with both boys. "I am your friend, though. And that's good enough. Now, let's ride Cupcake."

Like a miracle, Adam's tears dried, and Drew's smile reappeared. Gretchen, however, was another story, and she remained aloof.

The boys rode Cupcake a full twenty minutes before tiring. Ryder stood in the center of the pen, giving them instruction. Correction, giving Drew instruction. Adam sat behind his brother, holding on. Tatum couldn't resist and took several pictures with her phone. All right, she admitted it. She took a few shots just of Ryder. Who could resist?

"Time to get home, boys." Tatum scanned the area for Gretchen. Her daughter had found twin sisters to play with, children of Liberty's client. Confident her daughter was fine and adequately supervised, she returned her attention to Ryder.

"Let's unsaddle this steed." Ryder lifted first Adam, then Drew, off Cupcake.

"What's a steed?" Drew asked.

"A powerful horse."

"Cupcake's not powerful."

"Says who?"

While they were taking Cupcake to the barn, Mercer hailed Ryder. "There you are."

"You go on," Tatum said "I can unsaddle Cupcake."

He waved to his father and kept walking. "Be right there, Dad."

"Are you stalling?" She didn't intend to be blunt; the question had simply slipped out.

"A little."

"Is something wrong?"

"No." He took her arm as if to hurry her.

Under different circumstances, she'd have appreciated the sensation of his fingers firmly pressing into her flesh. Instead, her hackles rose. The past forty minutes had been simply a ruse.

"You don't have to use me, use the kids, as an excuse to avoid your family."

"Is that what you think?" Ryder asked.

Tatum's chin went up. "Frankly, yes."

They stopped outside the tack room. Drew held Cupcake's reins out of reach while Adam jumped up and down in place, crying, "Me, me, me."

"Okay, it's true. I am avoiding my family." Before she could offer a retort, he reached up and cupped her cheek. He didn't stop there and brushed the pad of his thumb along her bottom lip. "But I can't think of a better diversion."

Oh, to lean into his hand. Better yet, stand on her tiptoes and press her lips to his incredible mouth.

Steeling her resolve, she resisted. "Thank you. The boys appreciate it."

"I wasn't talking about them."

"Ryder." Her voice almost failed her.

"You're right." He let his hand drop. "Much as I'd like to explore possibilities, I can't. It wouldn't be fair."

"Because I work for your family?"

"That's one reason."

"I might not be an Easy Money employee for much longer if the school board approves the new budget."

"Let's see what happens." He patted Drew's head. "Come on, you two. I need help unsaddling this steed."

Tatum fought off the pain. Ryder hadn't exactly jumped for joy when she mentioned the possibility of returning to teaching. Why hadn't she kept her mouth shut? He might still be cupping her cheek.

RYDER AND HIS father sat in the rickety wooden stands. Third row. They were the sole spectators. The arena at the Lost Dutchman Rodeo Company in Apache Junction wasn't set up to accommodate official rodeo events. These stands were reserved strictly for customers, such as the Becketts, in order to observe the available bucking stock in action.

And they were getting a lot of action this morning. The five bulls they'd seen so far were all prize-winning and in their prime. No one could fault their quality or potential.

The final bull scheduled to view was, at that moment, being herded from the narrow runway into the bucking chute. He was a tough-looking Brahma crossbreed with a large dark patch on his hind end that, if one used imagination, resembled the shape of a closed fist. Ryder wondered if that was any indication of the bull's bucking abilities.

Slowly, the cowboy lowered himself onto the bull's back, his spotter straddling the wall beside him and ready to pull the flat braided rope that would tighten the cowboy's grip. Two other Lost Dutchman hands stood nearby, their boots on the bottom rung of the fence, arms slung over the top rail. If necessary, they'd jump in and pull the cowboy off, should, for any reason, the bull become agitated or threatening.

"Watch." Ryder's father nodded in the direction of the chute. "That brute will dive left the second he breaks free."

"You're wrong. He's going to buck."

"See him turning his head? He's setting his course."

"Nope. He's pawing the ground with his back left hoof."

An easy grin spread across his father's face. They'd disagreed like this before. Often. All in good sport. "Winner buys lunch?"

"Get your wallet out."

The wooden floorboard beneath Ryder's feet vibrated, alerting him of Donnie Statler's approach.

Though only in his late fifties, the owner of the Lost Dutchman moved like an eighty-year-old, as if every bone in his body screamed in agony. They probably did. A lifetime of rodeoing was hard on a man.

"What do you think so far?" Donnie slowly lowered himself onto the bleacher seat next to Ryder.

The three had chatted earlier when Ryder and his father arrived that morning. Donnie had taken them around to view the stock and given them a brief rundown on each bull, its history and potential. This was Ryder's first meeting with Donnie, though his father knew the man from back in the day and his many years as a bucking stock contractor. Ryder would have to be deaf and blind not to notice the tension between the two.

They were about the same age and had, from the stories they'd shared earlier, once competed against each other. Heatedly. Both in rodeoing and, as Donnie was quick to point out, for the attention of Ryder's mother—when they were on the circuit and later, after the divorce.

But Ryder didn't think a long-ago rivalry was the cause of the tension. At least for Donnie. Ryder's guess, and he'd bet money on it, was that Donnie didn't appreciate the competition from the Easy Money, which had increased with the recent purchase of their own bucking bulls.

And, yet, here they were, looking at bulls to lease for their Wild West Days Rodeo. Not in competition with the Lost Dutchman at all but as its customer.

Donnie gave Ryder's knee a friendly slap. One with remarkable strength. Apparently he wasn't in as much pain as he appeared. "You can take a spin on that fellow, if you have a hankering."

"Thanks." Ryder chuckled. "Been far too many years for me to try." Fifteen, to be exact.

"Like riding a bicycle, my friend. You never forget."

Ryder had his doubts. "Maybe we can start with something smaller."

"Got us a few young steers in the back."

"I was thinking more of that bike you mentioned."

The men indulged in a good laugh. A moment later, the tension resumed.

"Was a time you leased a whole lot more bulls from me," Donnie said.

Ryder's father was quick with a comeback. "For a while there, we didn't lease any."

That was true. After a bull-goring accident, which left an Easy Money cowboy permanently disabled, Ryder's mother sold off their entire herd. From then on, during the arena's four annual rodeos, she'd lease bulls from Donnie. It had been an agreeable and profitable arrangement for both parties, up until Ryder's father had returned and purchased six new bulls. It was his plan to purchase more.

Donnie chewed thoughtfully on an unlit matchstick. "I've come to count on the income. The loss will cut into my profits."

"That's the way of business."

Hearing his father's retort, Ryder wanted to elbow him in the ribs. The day might come when the Becketts didn't need the Lost Dutchman. Today wasn't it. With entries pouring in for the rodeo, they'd need a lot more than their six bulls. Donnie's were the best around and the least expensive to transport. Angering him would serve no purpose, even if he did seize every opportunity to goad Ryder's father.

"Look, Donnie," Ryder said. "You don't have us over a barrel, but you have us edged up against one. For the moment, we'd like to continue doing business with you."

The other man merely grunted.

Ryder's father smirked. "He's not the only bucking stock contractor in the state."

"I could call my mother," Ryder said. "I know you and she have always been able to come to terms."

Donnie broke out in a wide, gap-toothed grin and slapped Ryder's knee again. "Best idea you've had all day, young man."

His father's piercing glare could have melted titanium. "We can negotiate an agreement just fine without involving Sunny."

That was what Ryder thought all along.

Conversation came to a stop when the chute door opened, and the Brahma bull exploded into the arena, first, two, then, all four hooves off the ground.

Beside him, Ryder's father muttered, "Damn. Would've sworn that fellow'd go left."

Ryder had no time to savor his victory. Beating impossible odds, the cowboy hung on, even spurring the bull to greater heights. The Brahma twisted to the left, to the right, and to the left again before raising his hind feet an easy six feet off the ground.

The display was great while it lasted. An instant before the buzzer went off, the cowboy lost the battle and was launched into the air, sailing high over the bull's head. Having the sense to tuck himself into a ball, he landed well off to the side of the beast, which was quickly chased to the far end of the small arena and out the gate by two more Lost Dutchman hands. The cowboy was up and dusting off his jeans long before the hands reached him.

"*Puño* won't disappoint," Donnie observed.

Spanish for fist, Ryder thought. The mark on the bull's hind quarters. It was an appropriate name. "I don't think any of your stock will."

"Damn straight."

"We could use six more in addition to the ones we've seen, if you have that many available."

"Might." Donnie eyed him, the unlit matchstick bobbing up and down.

"Let's talk." Ryder rose and waited for the other man. Behind him, his father also stood. He half expected Mercer to insist on taking over. That didn't happen. Good. His father was showing some sense.

Ryder hadn't intended to assume control of the negotiations or step on his father's toes. But this was business. Not personal. He had no history with Donnie and wasn't about to lose sight of the bigger goal simply because his ego took a hit.

An hour later, Ryder and his father left the Lost Dutchman with a copy of their newly signed and dated commitment to lease.

"I'm hungry," his father said the moment he was behind the wheel. He'd insisted on driving. "Let's stop at the Flat Iron for that lunch I owe you."

Ryder didn't object and not only because he'd won the bet. Neither of them was much for cooking. If they didn't eat out at least one meal a day, they'd starve.

"You were good back there, son. I'm glad you tagged along."

"I am, too. If only to meet Donnie."

Originally, Ryder had thought he'd stay at the arena. The farrier was due this morning, and he'd wanted to inspect Cupcake. A pony's feet were small and different from a horse's, which no doubt accounted for the ill-fitting shoe in the first place. But Liberty said she'd inspect the farrier's work before paying him. Next to Ryder and his father, she was the best choice and most knowledgeable.

Just as well. Ryder wasn't sure another encounter with Tatum was a good idea under the circumstances. Seemed every time they were together, he either said or did something to give her the wrong impression.

His fault. She'd looked so vulnerable yesterday, he couldn't resist touching her. If only to assure her. Except, he'd done the opposite. She was more confused than ever. He'd be, too, if someone continued giving him mixed signals.

He expelled a long, slow breath. It had been worth it. Her skin was the color of gold and the texture of satin. He'd wanted to slide his palm from her cheek to her neck, then drive his fingers into that incredible hair. What might it look like fanned across his pillow? Better yet, across his naked chest.

Dangerous thoughts he'd best avoid. Tatum Mayweather's desires were written all over her face. Gold ring, white picket fence and good stepdad to her kids. Ryder would disappoint her, sooner if not later.

"Those terms you negotiated were good," his father said. "Better than our last contract with Donnie."

They were in the truck, heading back to Reckless.

"It was a simple contract, Dad. Tatum could have done just as well."

"She doesn't know the first thing about marketing or promotion. And she sure as heck doesn't know about bucking stock contracts."

"She might surprise you. Have you considered giving her more responsibility?"

"She's quitting and going back to teaching."

What would his father think if he found out that Ryder was working with a headhunter? He wouldn't be happy, that was for sure.

Ryder hadn't promised forever. That didn't mean his father and Liberty believed otherwise. She'd pressured him hard last night at dinner to reconcile with their mother, certain if he did, he'd stay. Ryder hadn't wanted to disappoint her, but he wasn't ready.

Three days home and he'd hardly seen or spoken to his mother, other than the homecoming lunch. She might be giving him time and space to come around. Ryder was choosing the path of least resistance.

"Three months."

"What?" Ryder shook his head to clear it.

"That's my target date," his father said. "To buy more bulls. Enough so that we don't have to lease any from the Lost Dutchman or anyone else. Also some heifers. Within a year, we'll start breeding and raising our own bucking stock."

"Then we *will* be in competition with Donnie."

"There's room enough for both of us. He's strictly a contractor. We have the arena. And he doesn't have your mother."

"Aren't you carrying an old jealousy a bit too far?"

"Not talking about that. Your mom's smart as a whip. She and I, we were unstoppable once. Going to be again."

What his parents did wasn't really any of his business.

Still, Ryder felt the need to caution his father. "Can you trust Mom?"

"Are you kidding? She's great with money."

"She threw you out."

"I deserved that. I was a drunk and hell-bent on bankrupting the arena."

"You didn't deserve it, Dad. People make mistakes. You have to quit defending her."

"If I'd have stayed, I might not have gotten sober. Sometimes you just have to cauterize the wound. Hurts like the dickens, but that's the only way it'll heal."

"All right."

"Your mother's not a bad person, son."

Ryder wasn't in the mood to debate. "I'll just shut up now."

"Is that why you haven't married? Because your mother and me couldn't make a go of it?"

"I was married."

"Not for long. And, as far as I can tell, there hasn't been anyone serious since. Hate thinking it's your mom's and my fault."

Ryder sat back and stared out the windshield. While he'd have liked to dismiss his father's question as nonsense, he couldn't and had asked himself the same thing more than once.

Putting his career first or not finding the right woman were his go-to replies when pressed about his bachelorhood. Could it be he didn't believe in the institution of marriage? Not only had he failed at it, so had his parents. Miserably. Their divorce had wound up dividing his entire family.

With that kind of history, anyone would be scared of commitment, even with a lovely and appealing woman like Tatum Mayweather.

Chapter Five

Tatum wore a skirt today but not because she and Ryder were scheduled to go over the current bucking stock contracts together. Absolutely not. Sometimes, she abandoned her customary jeans in favor of dressier clothes. Like when a representative from the regional office of the PCA visited the arena or during the annual liability insurance audit last month.

She tugged on the front of her skirt as she sat at her desk, making sure the material lay smooth. Right, who was she fooling? She'd totally dressed up for Ryder.

How could she be annoyed at him for sending out mixed signals when she wore an outfit meant to encourage signals? Just as well she hadn't seen much of him the past few days. The upcoming rodeo and the Easy Money's participation in Wild West Days was keeping them both busy. She'd heard from Liberty that he'd inspected Cupcake's new shoeing job and gave the farrier a passing grade.

That was a relief. She really should remember to thank him.

Glancing at the clock on the wall, something she'd been doing all day in anticipation of Ryder's arrival, she smoothed her skirt again. Not that it had wrinkled in the past five minutes.

Luckily, the phone rang, and she was temporarily distracted from stressing over what was nothing more than a work session between two fellow employees. She'd barely hung up when the Federal Express deliveryman arrived with a package. Tatum couldn't wait to see the contents. Placing the large box on her desk, she opened it and rifled through the packing material like a dog digging a hole.

Carefully, she removed the navy banner with its gold trim and silver lettering. It looked good, great even, and she allowed herself a moment's satisfaction.

Tatum had been put in charge of designing and ordering the new banner, the old one being a worn relic. She'd also convinced Sunny that, in order to be properly represented, the arena's logo needed a redesign. If it turned out terrible, Tatum would have borne the responsibility entirely.

But it hadn't, though she couldn't be a hundred percent sure until she saw the banner unfurled. With little room to maneuver, and not wanting to soil the fabric, she draped all eight feet of it across her desk. The ends hung over the sides, distorting the effect. She was just rethinking her approach when Ryder entered the office from the barn door.

"Nice," he commented, taking in the banner.

She could have said the same thing about him. In the week since his arrival, his clothes had gone from having that store-bought newness to casually comfortable. At first glance, he'd easily pass for one of the arena's regular hands. Any better looking and Tatum would do something stupid, like preen or swoon or—heaven forbid—flirt.

"I think so, too." She studied the banner, tapping her lower lip with her finger. "Just wish I could see all of it."

"Here." He grabbed one end and lifted it off her desk. "You get that side."

They stood opposite each other, the banner stretched between them.

"The logo's new." Ryder referred to the silhouette of a bucking horse kicking a dollar sign into the air. "I like it. Your design?"

"Yes." Tatum couldn't resist a grin.

"You're good."

A warm feeling bloomed inside her that had less to do

with his praise and more to do with the sexy timbre of his voice. *Stay strong*, she warned herself.

"I was worried it wouldn't get here in time for the parade," she said.

"Mom mentioned we have an entry."

As usual. Participating in the Wild West Days parade was a longstanding Beckett tradition.

"Will you be riding with the family?" Tatum moved toward him, folding the banner as she did.

Ryder did the same. "Doubtful."

"Why not?"

Many of the arena's students would accompany the Beckett family. They'd had to limit the number to the first thirty who'd signed up, the maximum parade regulations allowed. Two of the advanced students, astride their trustworthy horses, had been chosen to ride at the front of the group, each carrying one end of the banner. During the rest of the year, it would be used for the opening and closing ceremonies in their various rodeos and horse shows.

"We'll see," Ryder hedged.

"It'll be fun."

"Are you riding in the parade?" The tone of his voice made her think he'd change his mind if she were to say yes.

"No. But I'm taking my kids to watch. They love it."

"Maybe I'll see you there."

They finished folding and stood together, toe to toe. A small tingle of awareness climbed Tatum's spine. "Are you ready to start on the contracts?"

"Where's the best place to sit?"

Good question, and one that caused her awareness of him to escalate. The other day, he'd occupied a visitor chair, and they'd passed files back and forth over her desk. That arrangement wouldn't work today; he needed to see her computer screen. Why hadn't she thought of this before?

"Well, um…" She went to stand behind her desk, as if that vantage point would prompt an idea.

He suddenly lifted the visitor chair and carried it over to the cramped space beside her.

"It's a little tight," she observed.

It was a *lot* tight. Tatum scooted her chair to the right, creating maybe three extra inches.

"Luckily I showered today," Ryder said in jest before sitting.

Yeah. She'd noticed his crisp, fresh scent earlier. Lowering herself onto her chair, she strived for control by getting straight to business.

"Did you read the draft letter I emailed you yesterday?" She'd composed a follow-up contract for the secretary at the mining company.

"I did. Well worded."

Again, more praise delivered in that incredible voice of his. How had the female members of his team at the marketing firm been able to concentrate with him as their leader?

"Should I send it to her?"

"Include a discount coupon."

She nodded. "I've also been working on that list of potential companies for reciprocal advertising." She clicked on a document. "These are just for Arizona. I wasn't sure what other states you wanted to try."

"New Mexico, for sure. And southern California."

They'd finished with the list and were reviewing the current client roster when Sunny returned from giving potential new clients a tour of the grounds.

The look of concentration on Sunny's face vanished upon seeing Ryder. "Hi, honey." She came over, bent and kissed the top of his head.

The gesture was sweet and motherly and very much like one Tatum gave her own children. Only they didn't stiffen their jaw muscles.

"Hey, Mom." Ryder's neutral tone was in stark contrast to his mother's warm one.

Sunny's features fell. The next instant she composed

herself. "I see you're working. I won't bother you." She headed to her office. Fled was a better description.

Tatum bit her tongue. As bad as she felt for her boss, it wasn't her place to say anything. She also sensed Ryder wasn't one to be pushed. Any reconciliation would be on his terms.

Still, her heart ached. Ryder and Sunny weren't the only ones affected. All of the Becketts suffered along with mother and son. Did Ryder not see that?

An hour later, he and Tatum were knee deep in the bucking contract files. Where had the afternoon gone? Soon, she'd have to leave to pick up Gretchen from school and the boys from day care. Not Benjie. Cassidy had taken him out of class for a dentist appointment.

Ryder had made copious notes as they'd worked, his bold, strong strokes filling the pages. Several times, Tatum had to stop and answer the phone or deal with a customer. Ryder remained ever patient.

She was just explaining about the Haversons from the Shade Tree Arena in Wickenburg when the phone rang again. Only this time, it was her cell phone from her purse in the lower desk drawer.

Hmm. Most people knew better than to bother her during working hours. This was either a sales call or something important.

"Excuse me." She maneuvered her knees to the side in order to access the drawer. Naturally, that caused them to press against Ryder's. "It's my babysitter," she said, already starting to worry.

"Sorry to bother you," her sitter said in a rush. "It's Drew. He was playing kick ball in the yard with the other kids and hurt his finger."

"How bad is it?" Tatum imagined a cut or sprain.

"Bad. It's sticking straight out at this really weird angle. I'm pretty sure he broke it."

Without thinking, Tatum scrambled to her feet and

tried to push past Ryder, shaking badly enough she nearly dropped the phone. She did drop her purse. "I have to go. Drew's hurt."

Ryder blocked her exit. "I'll take you."

"I can't ask that of you."

"You're too upset to think straight, much less drive."

"Gretchen's out at three. She'll be waiting for me at the school."

He took her by the arm, his firm hold silencing any argument. "I'll pick her up after I take you and the boys to the clinic."

"What about Adam's car seat? Your truck—"

"Where's your car parked?"

"Behind the barn."

Over his shoulder he called, "Mom, I'm taking Tatum to pick up Drew. He's been hurt."

Sunny came rushing out. "Do you need anything? Is he all right?"

"A broken finger."

"You'd better hurry."

"I'm so sorry to leave you in a bind." Tatum swallowed a sob.

"Call me later," Sunny said.

"I will. I promise."

Ryder didn't let go of Tatum's arm until they reached her car.

Little by little, she relaxed. It had been a long time since she'd let a capable man take control. She could easily grow accustomed to the change.

FIRST, RYDER DELIVERED TATUM, Drew and Adam to the small medical clinic in town. Then, after Tatum made arrangements with the school, he picked up Gretchen and drove her to the clinic.

They spent exactly ten minutes there. The physician's assistant on duty could do no more for Drew's dislocated pinky finger than immobilize it, secure an ice pack to his hand with an elastic bandage and administer a mild pain reliever.

"You need to see a doctor," she advised. "To set the finger. Preferably an orthopedic surgeon."

At ten past four, they had no choice but to drive into Globe and wait in line at the hospital emergency room—along with countless other sick and injured individuals. Drew couldn't go the entire weekend with a dislocated finger.

Tatum fretted endlessly on the drive to Globe. About Drew, who thought his pinky protruding at a ninety degree angle was cool. About Adam, who fussed and whined because he'd missed his afternoon nap. About inconveniencing Ryder. About leaving abruptly and dumping her work on Sunny. About the costs and whether the health insurance would pay for an emergency-room visit. About whether she should call Monty or just wait.

"Take it easy," Ryder told her and reached across the seat to comfort her. When he would have removed his hand from hers, Tatum gripped his fingers and squeezed as if he alone was responsible for keeping her anchored in place.

He didn't complain and steered the car with his other hand.

"I'm trying." She glanced at Drew in the backseat, bracketed by Adam in the car seat on his right and a very grumpy Gretchen on his left. Apparently she was supposed to go to a friend's house after school. Tatum had admitted to forgetting about it in all the rush. "I should be glad it's relatively minor and something that will heal."

"He'll be fine. I've broken plenty of bones in my life. Survived every one."

"Rodeoing?"

"Most. A couple years ago, I busted my ankle playing second base at a company softball game. We lost anyway."

She offered up a weak smile.

"That's better," he said, wishing he could do more to ease her anxiety.

She released his fingers and rested her hands in her lap.

Damn. That had been nice. Sweet. Gentle. With his former coworker, intimacy had been for one purpose only, as if their relationship was too trivial to sustain any emotional depth. Was that why she'd been so angry at him for calling it off?

The line at the ER was long. Ryder's gaze traveled the entire length of the room, noting the majority of chairs were occupied. A teenaged girl in gym clothes held an ice pack to her collarbone. An elderly man with a crudely bandaged hand cursed the dog that bit him. In every corner of the room, adults and children alike coughed and hacked, fighting off the early flu bug going around.

Ryder guided their small group over outstretched legs to the only available seats. Tatum then read to, cajoled, rocked, and played games with her children in an attempt to keep them from fussing too much. An hour later, a nurse toting a clipboard called Drew's name.

"I want to go with Mommy," Gretchen complained when the nurse informed them that she and Adam weren't allowed in the examining area. "Not fair."

"I'm sorry to ask this." Tatum gave Ryder a pleading look.

"You just take care of Drew." Certainly, he could handle a two- and seven-year-old for a few minutes.

"You listen to Mr. Beckett, you hear me? Don't give him any trouble."

Adam ignored his mother and attempted to scale Ryder's knee. He had to help the boy the last foot into his lap. Gretchen pouted and plunked herself down on her seat, leaving an empty chair between her and Ryder. She still hadn't forgiven him for…to be honest, he wasn't sure what.

"But I don't want them to fix my finger," Drew moaned as Tatum led him by his good hand. "It's awesome."

They disappeared with the clipboard-carrying nurse though a double door.

"You want to color or something?" Ryder asked Gretchen. "There's some books over there." He had to crank his head sideways to see around Adam, who stood on Ryder's thigh, bouncing in place and talking up a storm in some kind of alien language. Geez, the kid was actually heavy, and his shoes were hard as concrete.

"I'm too old to color." Gretchen stared at the TV hanging on the wall playing an infomercial for a cleaning product. She couldn't possibly be interested in that.

"Okay."

She gave him an entire minute before demanding, "That's it?"

"I guess."

"You're supposed to ask me if I want to read a book or hear a story."

"I don't know any stories." Not any suitable for little girls.

She huffed. "I don't know why my mom likes you."

"She likes me?" Ryder really shouldn't have been so pleased by this revelation. But he was. Immensely. "Did she tell you that?"

Gretchen's response was to fold her arms across her middle, drop her chin to her chest and pout.

"Hungwee," Adam said and flung himself over Ryder's right shoulder.

"Sorry, pal. We're going to have to wait until your mom gets back." Ryder wondered if there was some way he could wrangle Adam off his lap and into the empty chair. The young man sitting across from Ryder and talking on his cell phone didn't look particularly happy about a loud, rambunctious kid in such close proximity.

"Hungwee," Adam shouted.

"There's a vending machine in the hallway." The suggestion came from a woman accompanying her sick friend. "You can probably find something for your son."

"He's not our daddy!" Gretchen turned pink with indignation.

"Oh." The woman drew back. "My mistake."

"No worries." Ryder stood, lifting Adam as he did. "Come on, big guy. You, too," he added when Gretchen didn't move.

"I'm staying."

Given her stubborn streak, he should have anticipated this. "You're not hungry?"

Interest flickered in her eyes.

"Hungwee," Adam bellowed directly into Ryder's ear, nearly deafening him.

Gretchen stood, one painstakingly slow inch at a time.

Finally. Another minute and Ryder's teeth would be ground to nubs.

"I can't eat anything with gluten in it," she announced.

There were exactly three items in the vending machine that met the gluten-free requirement.

"I hate corn nuts," she announced. "And peanuts."

Ryder inserted several dollar bills into the machine and pressed a button. "Corn chips it is."

She accepted them grudgingly.

"Does Adam like corn chips, too?"

"He's not supposed to have junk food."

That left few choices as the vending machine was loaded with junk food. Ryder selected some awful-looking orange crackers with yellow cheese for him.

"Aren't you hungry, too?" Gretchen asked.

Ryder moved to the next machine. "I'm having a soda."

"Mom says sodas are bad for you. They're full of sugar. Can I have a juice?"

The only non-soda selections were plain bottled water and vitamin water. Ryder bought two of the latter and a cola for himself. Hopefully, Tatum would approve of his choice, or at least, cut him some slack, given the circumstances.

When they returned to the waiting area, Gretchen sat next to Ryder—interesting—and ate in silence. Adam gobbled three crackers and drank half his vitamin water, some of which spilled on to his clothes, then promptly fell asleep atop Ryder.

Ten minutes into the nap, Ryder's left arm went numb. He shifted Adam to the other side. The boy, out like a light, didn't so much as twitch an eyelash.

Gretchen had finished her chips. Ryder pretended not to notice when she got up and ambled toward the table in the corner with the coloring books and crayons.

His cell phone rang three times. The first call was from Cassidy, wanting an update. Ryder spoke softly, not wanting to wake up Adam.

"Haven't heard yet. They're back with the doctor."

"Poor Tatum. She doesn't need another problem."

"She seems to be hanging in there."

"What about Gretchen and Adam?"

"She's coloring and he's sleeping." Ryder shifted the boy again, this time laying him across his lap like a rag doll.

"How did you wind up driving them to Globe?"

"Tatum was upset, and I was there."

"Hmm. Well, okay. Seems like you have everything handled." Her tone revealed surprise and—could it be?—a hint of admiration. "Tell Tatum to call me when she has a minute."

The third call came from Myra Solomon. "I've already generated some buzz about you. There's a firm in Denver showing interest."

"That's great." Ryder's enthusiasm was several degrees lower than he'd expected.

"Can you get here now to film that video interview? We'll stay late."

He was supposed to have gone in yesterday for the video

interview but had stalled Myra. He knew his next answer would disappoint her.

"I can't. I'm at the ER with a friend. Her son injured himself playing kick ball."

"Ryder." The headhunter's warning was unmistakable. "You can't put this off any longer."

"First thing, Monday morning. I promise."

"I'd better see your smiling face here by nine a.m. on the dot."

"You will." That gave him two days to come up with an excuse for his absence from the Easy Money. The family was bound to notice.

Finally Tatum and Drew emerged through the door, a different nurse accompanying them. Drew's hand was heavily bandaged, the finger no longer sticking out, and his arm in a sling. His earlier glee had disappeared. In fact, he looked as if he'd been crying. Setting the finger must have hurt.

As they approached, Ryder could hear the young man going over Drew's discharge instructions with Tatum. If her streaked mascara was any indication, she'd been crying, too.

"Read everything carefully. Doctor recommends using over-the-counter liquid children's acetaminophen. If his pain is acute, call this number, and he'll prescribe something stronger. Rest and confinement for the next few days. No strenuous activity for a month."

"Yay!" Drew's glee returned. "I get to stay home from day care," he singsonged.

"We'll see, baby. Mommy still has to work." Tatum accepted the stack of papers from the nurse, and he departed. She took one look at Adam, slung limply across Ryder's lap, and came to a stop. "Oh. Sorry about that."

Ryder shrugged. "Better he's sleeping than crying."

"Was he crying?"

"I gave him orange crackers and vitamin water. If he's sick, it's all my fault."

"He's eaten worse and survived. Once I caught him in the pantry, shoving fistfuls of kitty kibble into his mouth." Tatum brushed at her cheeks.

His heart went out to her. "Was it tough watching the doctor set the finger?"

Ryder remembered a time when he'd fallen from their pony Flame. The cut on his chin had required sixteen stitches. His mother had carried on worse than him. In the end, he'd wound up comforting her.

Why should he remember that now?

"He's so young," was Tatum's only answer.

Gretchen managed to drag herself away from the coloring table. Fists balanced on her hips, she glared at Drew and demanded, "Let me see your cast."

"It's not a cast." He sounded disappointed. "Just a…a…"

"Splint," Tatum said. She turned to Ryder. "He sees the orthopedic surgeon on Monday."

Drew brightened. "Then I get a cast. I want a green one." He stared up at Tatum. "Mommy, I'm hungry.

"Me, too." Gretchen sidled up to Tatum and clutched her free hand.

She smiled apologetically at both her children. "We have to get Drew's medication at the store first, sweetie, then head home. We've taken up enough of Mr. Beckett's time."

Gretchen made a face.

Ryder gently lifted Adam and stood. Without thinking too much about it, he held the still-sleeping boy against his chest. The kid stirred, wrapped his small arms around Ryder's neck, and promptly drifted back to sleep. Ryder absently patted the boy's back.

"There's a drugstore in the shopping center across the street. Also a fast-food chicken place. Everyone like fried chicken?"

"Yes!" Drew raised his good arm in a fist pump.

"I can't have fried chicken," Gretchen said grumpily.

Tatum patted her head. "She's gluten intolerant. There's breading—"

"I heard," Ryder said. "We can go somewhere else."

"It's fine, sweetie. The restaurant has baked chicken, too."

As they were leaving, a nurse came out and called the name of the sick woman. Before her friend left with her, she leaned close to Ryder and said, "You may not be their father, but you'd make a good one."

Tatum obviously heard for a strange look came into her eyes, and she said nothing on their walk to the car.

Chapter Six

Food clearly worked wonders, as far as Tatum's brood was concerned anyway. Adam woke up from his nap in time to demolish a plate of mashed potatoes, a biscuit and carefully cut-up pieces of chicken. Gretchen complained about her lack of gluten-free choices but was pacified with the promise of dessert. Ryder's suggestion, and a good one if he did say so himself.

Drew, Ryder's new best buddy, sat close to him and practically inhaled his food. Tatum rode herd on them all, serving up portions and wiping messy hands and faces with paper napkins.

"Aren't you going to eat?" Ryder asked, noticing she'd hardly touched her food.

"I will." She took a single bite, then became distracted when Adam dropped his straw on to the floor and began to wail. She grimaced. "I'm sorry. Really I am."

"It's okay, Tatum. They're just being kids."

"And you like kids."

"I like yours."

He found her expression difficult to interpret. Was she pleased or irritated with him? The next instant, she turned away.

The thing was, her kids really didn't bother him. The boys were great. A typical rough-and-tumble pair. And Gretchen? Well, she wasn't so bad when she let that damnable guard of hers down. It was to be expected, really. She'd been through a lot in recent years. Her parents divorcing, the family moving—twice—and then being shipped off to her grandmother's for four months. That would put anyone on the defensive.

They made it back to Reckless at about seven-thirty. Tatum had placed several phone calls during the drive. To Drew's father. Her babysitter. Cassidy. And, lastly, her sister in Tucson. Everyone was relieved to hear Drew's dislocation wasn't worse.

Ryder paid extra close attention when she spoke with Monty, listening while pretending not to. He heard resentment and also frustration. Monty, it seemed, wasn't overly concerned that his son was hurt. Only because she'd insisted, he talked to Drew. Tatum handed her phone over the seat and stared out the window during the entire brief conversation.

At the arena, Ryder pulled into a space near the office. He and Tatum exited the car and met up near the rear bumper. Night had fallen during the ride home, but overhead floodlights lit up the arena like a small city while leaving other places in shadows. Such as where Ryder and Tatum stood.

A group of local barrel racers had reserved the arena and were having practice runs. Spectators applauded as a young woman galloped her horse around the course, dirt exploding at each turn.

Ryder didn't see any of his family, but he suspected some of them, if not all, were in the vicinity.

"Thanks again for everything." Tatum lifted her gaze to Ryder's. "You went above and beyond today."

"It was fun."

"Right." She smiled. For the first time all day.

"And different," he conceded.

"That, I'll believe." The corners of her mouth drooped. "You must be exhausted."

"It has been a long day. And it's not over."

"See you tomorrow?"

"Not likely." She glanced toward the arena and sighed. "It's the weekend. I have art classes all day Saturday. Though sometimes we take Cupcake out for a ride on Sunday afternoons."

He'd forgotten about her not being there on the weekends. Less than a week home, and already he'd fallen into the habit of seeing her on a daily basis. What would happen when he left? Suddenly, he didn't want the evening to end.

"If you need a hand with the kids, just give me a—"

He was rendered speechless by her lips pressing against his cheek. Her touch was both gentle and electrifying. Closing his eyes, he let himself experience the moment.

Don't stop. Not yet.

She must have read his thoughts for she lingered. And lingered.

Her proximity brought with it a heat that invaded his every pore. As did the fragrant scent of her hair. Or was it the lotion she'd used that morning? Not to mention the silky texture of her skin.

Skin? Wait a minute.

Without realizing it, he'd lifted a hand to caress her bare arm.

She made the slightest move to pull away. Ryder would have none of it and drew her close. Closer still. He didn't stop until she was forced to grab hold of his shoulders or risk losing her balance.

"Ryder," was all she got out before he covered her mouth with his, turning a not-quite-innocent peck into a full-blown, make-no-mistake-I-want-you kiss.

She resisted for several seconds before relenting. He groaned low in his throat when she went soft and pliant in his arms.

With very little urging from him, she parted her lips. When his tongue entered her mouth, she answered his bold strokes in kind. Ryder gripped her harder, every one of his senses compelling him to take the kiss further and show her exactly what she did to him. How she made him feel.

It wasn't to be, however. Much, much too soon she withdrew, murmuring, "We can't. The children."

"Okay." He'd forgotten all about them.

Ryder was reluctant to let her go, though he knew he should. Had to. Must.

"That was…" Her voice fell away.

"Don't say a mistake, Tatum. Because it wasn't."

"I'm vulnerable. And you're being sweet."

"I kissed you because it's all I've been thinking of for days."

She sighed. "I'm an overworked single mom with three kids capable of driving a saint to sin. Which, after today, I'm thinking you are."

"Hardly." If she knew the kind of thoughts he was entertaining about her, him and a dark, secluded bedroom, she'd realize just how far he was from being a saint. "You're an incredibly attractive, very sexy lady, who also happens to be a great mother. I admire you, Tatum."

"Mom!" Gretchen stuck her head out the window. "Drew says his finger hurts."

"They're getting restless." Tatum eased away.

Ryder let his hand slide from her arm to her hand. Their fingers linked momentarily before parting for good. He walked out from behind the car and watched her leave. Drew and Adam waved to him through the backseat window. Gretchen simply stared. Had she seen him and her mother kissing?

Tatum also waved, an expression of uncertainty on her face. With good reason. He hadn't given her sufficient reason to expect that theirs was a relationship with a future.

Ryder turned to see his mother approaching. She also wore a look of uncertainty. His hope that she hadn't witnessed him and Tatum kissing was instantly dashed with her next words.

"I couldn't be happier that you're home, Ryder. But not at the expense of hurting that poor girl. She's gone through hell, and I don't want you putting her through any more."

RYDER'S FIRST REAL conversation with his mother since his return and what was it about? Him defending his actions to her.

She'd requested, insisted, really, that he accompany her to the announcer's booth above the bucking chutes, stating she hadn't locked up for the night. It was an excuse. She wanted them to be alone for the lecture she delivered. Possibly deserved. Nonetheless, his hackles rose.

"I'm not blind, Ryder. That was no kiss between friends."

Denying it would waste his breath and insult his mother's intelligence.

"Tatum doesn't date much, and I'm sure she kisses men even less." His mother flipped switches, powering down the equipment. The floodlights would remain on until the barrel racers were finished with their practice. During the weekends, which included Friday nights, that could last until ten or later. "She likes you. She always has. Which makes her susceptible to misreading your intentions."

"I happen to like her, too."

"In *that* way?"

"I'll be careful not to hurt her." Would he? He hadn't been thus far.

"She's vulnerable, Ryder, and takes matters of the heart very seriously."

He didn't answer right away, his concentration focused on the booth's interior with its large open window and bird's-eye view.

It had been a lot of years since Ryder was here. As little kids, he and Cassidy would pretend they were calling out events for a rodeo. Their mother would turn on the PA system, allowing their voices to carry across the entire property. Often, their father was in the arena, riding a horse or roping a calf.

Good times. He'd forgotten until right now. Another fond memory added to the list of ones he'd pushed aside when his parents divorced.

"She's walking a particularly fine line right now." The censure in his mother's voice returned Ryder to the present. "She had to leave her kids with her ex-mother-in-law for a while after she lost her job at the school and only recently got them back."

"Cassidy told me."

"It was difficult for her."

"I get it, Mom. I won't take advantage of her."

Yet, hadn't he done exactly that? Tatum may have made the first move, but that peck on the cheek was nothing more than a platonic thank-you. He'd taken the kiss to an entirely new level.

And she'd responded. Incredibly. Beautifully. If he closed his eyes, he could still feel her lips on his, her mouth opening in invitation. The gentle slope of her back as he trailed his hand down her spine. Her limbs becoming liquid as their kiss lingered and deepened.

How was it she didn't have droves of suitors beating down her door? And if she did, how would he feel about that?

Angry and territorial, though he'd have no right.

"I wouldn't worry," he said. "I doubt she's interested in me beyond a passing attraction."

"I agree."

Did she? Ryder staved off the blow to his ego.

"Monty wasn't the family-man type. He and Tatum gave it a go, but as soon as she had Gretchen, the marriage started to fail." She eyed him critically. "You're not the family-man type either."

"How would you know?"

At his brusque tone, she faltered. "You've been single for years. I assumed."

"For the record, you assumed wrong."

She looked stricken. "Sorry. My mistake."

Guilt pricked at him. He supposed it wasn't such a far-fetched conclusion. In the thirteen years since his divorce, he hadn't come anywhere close to settling down.

Not unlike his sister Cassidy. She, more so than him, shunned marriage. Even getting pregnant hadn't changed her mind. She insisted on raising Benjie alone without ever telling the father.

Ryder had long ago decided there were only two reasons for his sister's secrecy. Either the guy was married and she'd had an affair, or he was someone the Becketts would disapprove of.

He'd also decided it wasn't fair of his sister to deny Benjie the right to know his father, or for the father to know his son, whether or not the man was married. Their mother had done the same thing to Liberty—which probably explained why Cassidy believed there was nothing wrong with it. Could his family be more dysfunctional? Amazing, really, that Liberty had found love with a great guy and was headed to the altar. Perhaps she'd forgiven their mother for the lies.

"It's getting late, Mom." He started for the door.

"Wait, Ryder."

"I think we've covered everything we need to."

"If the school board doesn't approve the new budget and rehire Tatum, she'll be devastated. I'm not sure she can take another personal blow."

"Is there a chance she won't be hired back?"

"The board isn't in agreement on the budget. We meet again the week after next for the official vote."

"You'll keep her on here, won't you?"

"Of course. For as long as she wants."

"She's capable of more. There's nothing I've done this week she couldn't handle with minimal training."

"I disagree. You cut a good deal with Donnie for those bulls. Tatum hasn't ever been involved in contract negotiations."

"She's smart."

"She's also a little shy when she's in unfamiliar circumstances."

"Maybe she can shadow me next time." The idea appealed to Ryder.

His mother hesitated. "I'm not sure your father will go for that."

He'd gotten the same impression when talking to Mercer. "Why doesn't he like her?"

"That's not it at all. He wants you to stay. Training Tatum to do your job makes you dispensable."

"I didn't commit long-term when I agreed to help out."

"He's hoping to change your mind." She moved as if to touch him, then withdrew her hand. "I want you to stay, too."

"Why?"

"You're my son."

"Besides that?"

"The Easy Money is a family business, and you're part of the family."

"If Dad hadn't wormed his way back into the business, would you have still wanted me to be part of it?"

She appeared offended by his question. "Of course."

"You never said so."

"You had your job at Madison-Monroe. I didn't think you'd accept if I'd asked."

She was right about that.

Hand on the doorknob, he paused. There was one question he needed answered before ending this conversation. "Didn't you feel the least bit bad about lying to Liberty, to all of us, for years?"

"I felt terrible."

He chuckled derisively. "Not enough to tell the truth."

"I made a decision. I thought it was the right one at the time. If you're a parent one day, and I truly hope you are, then maybe you'll understand."

"Dad has been sober for twenty-two years. You don't think he proved himself a long time ago?"

"I was afraid."

"It's always about you, isn't it?"

"I did what I had to in order to protect my family."

Cassidy had said almost the exact same thing. Did she and their mother compare notes? Decide what they'd tell him? The thought irritated him. Ryder didn't like being played.

"You should know, I'm in talks with a headhunter."

Her expression instantly fell. "I wish you'd give this, the arena, us, a fair shot before deciding."

"I doubt it would make a difference."

She stiffened. "It certainly won't make a difference with that kind of attitude."

"Good night, Mom." Ryder left the booth and headed down the stairs. Reaching the bottom he strode briskly toward the barn, his mother's anguished face refusing to leave him.

He'd hurt her with his words. It was, after all, what he'd intended. She'd hurt him, too. Then and now.

The feeling of satisfaction he'd been counting on didn't come. Instead, he wanted to throw something. Or, better, punch a hole in a wall.

He did neither. He left the arena, taking the long way to his father's place.

Chapter Seven

Ryder parked his truck along Center Avenue, Reckless's main thoroughfare. As they were every weekend, parking spaces were at a premium. He'd have to walk a quarter mile to reach Tatum's art studio where Benjie was attending Saturday-morning class.

Cassidy had been busy with the barrel racers and unable to get away, their practice heating up in preparation for the upcoming Wild West Days Rodeo. Since he had another errand in town, Ryder had offered to pick up Benjie. After a brief hesitation, and a promise from Ryder that no harm would come to her son, she'd relented.

In truth, he was glad for the chance to have some one-on-one with his nephew. He really didn't know Benjie well and wanted to spend as much time as possible with him before he left.

At the corner, Ryder waited for the light to change and stifled a yawn. The talk with his mother had stayed with him long after it ended, interrupting his sleep. He kept telling himself he was right, his mother wrong. Experience had shown him, however, there were always two sides to every story. He had only to look at his termination from Madison-Monroe for proof of that.

As he strolled through town, he couldn't help noticing the many changes in preparation for the coming week. Wild West Days was a fever the locals had caught.

A white banner with bold red letters announcing the event was draped from one side of the street to the other.

Decorations adorned storefronts. Sandwich-board signs outside restaurants advertised specials, such as cowboy steaks and TexMex chili. An area had been cordoned off near the town square for Saturday night square dancing. Carpenters had assembled a wooden judge's stand outside the library. Mock weddings would be performed in front of the judge, and people arrested and charged with outlandish crimes. The wedding license fees and fines would then be donated to the library's book fund.

The summer before Ryder had moved in with his father, he'd been old enough to perform in the "shoot-outs," playing a bandit who was "gunned down"' as he tried to escape. He'd milked his role for all it was worth, showing off in front of his pals and, to be honest, a girl or two, with his Oscar-worthy performances.

Reaching the Silver Dollar Pawn Shop, a local establishment founded in the early 1900s that catered to both locals and tourists, he went inside. The store's wares included everything from rare Western antiques to jewelry to the latest electronic gadget. His upcoming video interview at Myra's office had spurred an idea for the arena, one that took hold last night and wouldn't let go. The Silver Dollar seemed a good place to start.

"Howdy!" The elderly woman behind the counter greeted him with a friendly smile. Four feet eleven in her shoes, she looked every bit of her seventy-plus years. "Can I help you with something in particular?" The friendly smile promptly blossomed. "Ryder. Ryder Beckett." She darted around the counter, nimble and chipper as an elf. "My, my, it's good to see you."

"Mrs. Danelli."

"Welcome home." She propelled herself at him, and he enveloped her petite frame in a fond embrace. "How are you?"

"I'm good. Sure is nice to see you."

They exchanged pleasantries for several minutes. Of

course, she'd heard about his return. Reckless was still a small town, and news traveled fast. She didn't ask why he'd quit his highfalutin marketing job, but he supposed she was curious like everyone else.

"I actually stopped in for a reason," he said. "Do you, by chance, carry any camcorders?"

"Several. Anything specific in mind?" She led him to an aisle in the store.

"I don't know a lot about them, but I'm looking for something professional and good quality."

"Really good?"

"Depends on the price."

"There was a gentleman who came in a few months ago. Claimed he was a filmmaker. Nature documentaries. Looking for money to finance a project. I wasn't sure I believed him or if I'd even take his equipment. Not much call for the high-end stuff. When he didn't come back to get his equipment out of hock, I doubted his story even more. When I called a few associates in the business, they told me the camcorder was actually one of the better ones on the market for that price range."

She unlocked the cable anchoring the merchandise to the shelf and handed the device to Ryder. It was larger than the handheld models he was used to seeing. A large microphone was attached to the top beside an elongated lens.

"There's a tripod and a case and some other accessories in the storage room. I didn't put them out. If you're interested, I'll find them."

"I'm interested."

Mrs. Danelli reappeared a few minutes later. She dropped the box on the counter, evidently as far as she could carry it. Ryder rifled through the contents while she assisted a newly arrived customer. Luckily, the original owner's manual was still in the case. He quickly scanned it.

"What do you think?" She sidled up next to him, the top of her permed gray hair barely reaching his shoulder.

Ryder replaced the charger he'd been inspecting in the box. "I'll take it."

She gave him a deal, and Ryder thanked her.

"Filming the rodeo this weekend?"

"And the different events around town." Ryder had a friend who was an editing genius and could probably take all the lousy footage he produced and turn it into a decent commercial short. Another friend could supply the voice-over. Perks of being in the marketing business for over a decade. "I'm hoping to make a digital short on the arena. For advertising."

"That's a great idea!"

And right up Ryder's alley. Much more so than delivering posters. Plus, his family could continue to use the digital short long after he left.

Mrs. Danelli sent him off with another hug and motherly peck on the cheek. Outside, he stood a moment and checked the time. Still ten minutes before art class was over. Cassidy had warned Ryder not to show up early. Her son was the class clown, and Ryder's presence would only give Benjie an excuse to cut up.

Hearing a loud clacking, Ryder spun. A riderless horse galloped straight for him, reins flapping and stirrups bouncing with each thunderous stride. Someone screamed. People dived out of the way like pins being knocked down by a bowling ball.

Horses weren't uncommon on the streets of Reckless, especially during Wild West Days. Uncontrolled horses, however, presented a danger.

Ryder didn't stop to think. He set the box with the camcorder on the sidewalk and ran into the street, arms waving and shouting, "Whoa. Whoa there, fellow."

For a split second, he thought the enormous bay gelding might gallop past him. All at once, it gathered its front hooves under it and clamored to a stop, eyes wide, nostrils flaring and flanks heaving.

Ryder gathered the reins and gripped them firmly just beneath the horse's jaw. "Easy does it. That's a good boy."

Whatever had spooked the horse seemed to have passed and, little by little, he calmed. Where was his rider, and was the man or woman all right? Ryder searched the vicinity but saw no one. Eventually, people ventured back on to the streets.

"Anyone know who this guy belongs to?" Ryder called out.

A few folks shook their heads or offered a "No clue," before walking away.

An old-timer wandered over. "That looks like one of Bucky Hendriks's stock. His crew has been in town since early this morning carousing and causing a ruckus. They're a good bunch of boys. Usually. Just get carried away now and then."

"You know where they are?"

"Last I heard, the Reverie."

A bar three blocks over. Strange that the horse's owner hadn't come to fetch him yet. Perhaps he was still inside the bar and unaware.

Ryder checked his watch again. Not enough time to take the horse to the bar and be back to fetch Benjie. But he could hardly abandon the bay, even tied up.

"You have a vehicle?" he asked the old-timer.

"My scooter."

Ryder noticed the motorized chair parked nearby. "You think you can drive it all the way to the Reverie?"

The man snorted with disdain, evidently insulted.

"Let Bucky's crew know I have the horse, and I'll be at the Ship-With-Ease Store. They can find him there."

The old-timer pressed pedal to the metal and took off at a brisk four miles an hour.

The horse perked his ears and stared after the man as if he, too, found the sight amusing.

"Let's go, boy."

Ryder gave the horse's neck a pat, then reached down, retrieved his box and balanced it in the crook of his arm. The horse ambled quietly beside him. They garnered their share of curious glances.

Outside the Ship-With-Ease Store, he stopped and tethered the horse to a wooden column.

Three young mothers stopped, glanced at the store and then Ryder.

"Ladies." He tugged on the brim of his hat, assuming they were parents of Tatum's students.

"Can we pet the horse?" one of them asked.

"Just be careful you don't move too fast."

Ryder heard a sudden bang behind him. Benjie stood at the art studio's large window, both palms and his nose pressed to the glass. Ryder could hear a muffled, "Hi, Uncle Ryder." A moment later, Drew materialized beside Benjie. The two pointed at him and broke into giggles.

Not good, Ryder thought. He could already hear the reprimand from Tatum.

As if on cue, she came up behind the boys. For a second, her gaze connected with his. Before he could mouth the words, *I'm sorry*, she marched the two young troublemakers away.

"Don't worry. She never stays mad for long."

Ryder faced the store owner, who'd come outside. "How you doing, Mr. Faust?"

The two men shook hands. "'Bout time you called me Lenny, I'd say."

For over thirty years, the older man had served as the town's postmaster. Forced into what he'd called an early retirement, he'd opened the Ship-With-Ease Store and proceeded to do a booming business, essentially competing with his former employer.

"Afraid I'm being a distraction," Ryder explained.

"Ah. Breaking the cardinal rule."

"Tatum's a good teacher, I hear."

"Great with them kids. Shame she lost her job at the school. If I have my way, she'll be teaching third grade again starting with the spring quarter."

"You have some sway with the board?"

"I'm one of the members. Serve with your mother. I'll be at the meeting next week."

"She didn't mention it."

"We're up against some strong opposition. Money is tight this year. The school doesn't have a lot to go around. Be a real shame to lose her."

"Do you think the board won't approve the budget increase?"

"Truthfully, I doubt the increase will pass." He sighed expansively. "Sunny and I, we're gonna do our best for that girl. Classrooms are crowded enough as it is. We need good teachers."

Ryder watched Tatum through the window. With the exception of her son and his nephew, every child stared at her with rapt attention. "She has a way with kids," Lenny echoed. "That's for sure. I told her she can use that space as long as she'd like. I'm not doing anything with it. Thought about expanding at one time, just hasn't happened. Don't really care about the extra rent money."

"That's nice of you."

More parents had gathered as they talked, the group swelling to the size of a small crowd. Ryder had a hard time keeping them away from the horse. In hindsight, he probably should have tethered the gelding farther from the art studio.

"I like that gal," Lenny said. "Heart of gold. I'm thinking you like her, too."

Did it show? "She's a good friend of my sister's."

He winked. "If that's what you say."

"I'm just here to pick up my nephew."

"Right."

Ryder was spared further scrutiny when the door to the

studio flew open, and the boys tumbled out on to the sidewalk. They were followed by eight or nine other children of similar ages.

"What are you doing with that horse, Uncle Ryder?" Benjie was the image of his mother, looks-wise. Personality-wise, they couldn't be more opposite. Whereas Cassidy was reserved and intense, Benjie was outgoing, boisterous and extremely social.

Was he like his father? Ryder found himself again wondering about the man's identity and why his sister kept it a secret. Did Benjie ever ask? What did she tell him?

"I kind of found him. His owner should be here any second." Ryder ruffled his nephew's already disheveled hair, then turned his attention to Drew. "How's the finger?"

"Mom says I'm brave."

"She's right."

His face fell. "I can't play kick ball. Or go swimming. Not until the cast is off."

"Would ice cream help? I can take you boys to Cascade." The ice cream parlor had been Ryder's favorite place as a kid.

"Yes!" Benjie and Drew exchanged high fives.

"I'll ask my mom." Drew would have darted back inside, but Tatum chose that moment to come out. He practically collided with her. "Mr. Beckett is taking us to Cascade!"

Tatum gave Ryder "the look." "Oh?"

"You're welcome to come with us. In fact, I'd like that."

"I have another class."

"You're on break," Drew said. "You just told us."

"I can watch the horse," Lenny offered.

Ryder grinned. "It's settled, then."

"Well," Tatum hedged.

"Please, Mom," Drew begged.

She pulled out a ring of keys and locked the door, relenting with a sigh.

"We won't be long." Ryder nodded at Lenny.

The older man winked again. "If that's what you say."

CASCADE ICE CREAM PARLOR wasn't far. Just up the street. Tatum ran herd on the boys, which was worse than corralling jackrabbits. They insisted on charging ahead, zigging first in one direction and zagging in the other. Leaving the art studio, even for a half hour, felt a little strange to her. Leaving with Ryder, stranger still. People were surely looking at them. Jumping to conclusions.

"Don't go far," she called after the boys.

They didn't listen.

Ryder walked casually along beside her. "Where are Gretchen and Adam?"

"At home with their grandmother." Tatum's reply was issued through clenched teeth. These days, any discussion of her former mother-in-law set her on edge. "She was going to take Drew, too, but he insisted on coming with me."

She didn't add that Drew pitched a fit when she told him he'd be spending the entire day with his grandmother. Try as she might, Tatum couldn't convince her oldest son that he'd be returned to her and not forced to live with his grandmother again. When his protests had dissolved into a fit of tears, Tatum had given in.

Her mother-in-law blamed her, of course. Accused her of spoiling Drew. She also blamed Tatum for the dislocated finger. The day care accommodations she'd chosen clearly weren't safe, if a child could suffer such a serious injury.

Tatum tried to tell herself that her mother-in-law's criticisms came from a place of love. She cared deeply for her grandchildren and wanted only the best for them. The problem was, beneath the caring and criticisms were subtle threats.

Mess up again, and you'll be hearing from Monty's attorney.

Not going to happen. Tatum refused to let it. She might not be living in the lap of luxury, but she was hardly an unfit parent.

"Is she visiting?" Ryder asked.

"For the day. It's a compromise."

Her gaze strayed to his profile. What would her mother-in-law think of her having ice cream with a man? A very good-looking one. Or of her kissing him? Tatum still couldn't believe she'd succumbed so easily.

She should tell Drew to say nothing about their trip to the ice cream parlor. Knowing her oldest son, he'd brag to Gretchen the first opportunity. Then, Tatum would have to explain.

Tension lay like a lead ball in the pit of her stomach.

"You and she compromise a lot?"

Glancing at Drew, Tatum assured herself that he and Benjie were occupied and not listening.

"Ruth comes to Reckless one Saturday a month, and I take the kids to see her one Sunday a month. In exchange, she doesn't pressure Monty to file for joint custody. Not that he wants it. He hardly ever visits the kids."

"Then, why?"

"Other than he typically does his mother's bidding?" Tatum swallowed. It did little to alleviate the bitter taste in her mouth. "She…questions my ability to provide adequately for my children."

"Because you lost your job at the school?"

"I went through a difficult financial period. We, um, had to move from a house to a three-bedroom apartment." She skipped over the part where she'd moved to a one-bedroom apartment for several months because that was all she could afford.

"Lots of people live in an apartment."

"Apparently not *her* grandchildren. I'm hoping to find a house to rent soon."

"When you go back to teaching?"

"Yes." And when she finally paid off the bulk of her credit card debt.

"Do teachers earn more than office managers?"

Tatum felt her cheeks flame. As a member of the Beckett

family, Ryder had access to payroll information and probably knew her weekly wage. In addition, he and his parents had met several times during the past week to discuss the monthly finances and income projections.

"There are also the benefits to consider," she said. "Retirement. Health insurance. Paid holidays. Your family does the best they can," she quickly amended. "Don't get me wrong."

"I understand. Believe me."

She hadn't stopped to consider until now that he'd probably given up a lot of benefits, too, when he quit his marketing job. Not for the first time, she questioned why he'd left such a good position.

"I realize the school may not rehire me, but I can't help hoping." And praying, she silently added.

"What if you were to be promoted at the Easy Money? You'd get a raise."

"Promoted." She suppressed a laugh. "To what? Sunny is the only other person in the office, and I don't think she's going anywhere."

"You could take on more of the marketing and promotion responsibilities."

"That's your job."

"For the time being." He shrugged. "Who knows what the future holds?"

His careless tone gave her pause. "Are you thinking of leaving the Easy Money?"

"Sooner or later."

It wasn't her place to ask, but she did anyway. "Have you told your family?"

"They know I'm not planning to stay indefinitely."

And they probably didn't like it. Mercer especially. According to Cassidy, Ryder and his mother argued last night. Was that what he meant by "sooner?"

As usual, the Becketts weren't getting along. Nothing cut a visit short like a family feud.

At Cascade's, they perused the many selections. Ryder took a long time deciding. Tatum always had the same thing. A single scoop of fat-free vanilla frozen yogurt. She was definitely a creature of habit.

Then again, she'd broken routine several times this past week. Wearing nice clothes to work. Relying on Ryder's help with Drew's emergency-room visit. Leaving the art studio during her break. Letting him kiss her. Kissing him back.

"What'll you have?" the fresh-faced teenaged clerk asked when the customers ahead of them moved on.

The boys wanted double scoops with two different flavors of ice cream, lots of syrup and sprinkles. Tatum grimaced just thinking about it.

When they were done, Ryder gestured, indicating she should order ahead of him. The words issuing from her mouth surprised her. "A double scoop of chocolate brownie fudge."

"Cone or dish?" the teen asked.

Tatum hesitated. The calories would go straight to her hips and live there forever.

"Don't hold back now," Ryder urged, a twinkle lighting his eyes.

"Cone."

"I'll have the same. And make it those waffle cones dipped in chocolate."

She would surely regret this. "They'll have to roll us out of here."

"What's the point of having ice cream if you don't make a pig of yourself?"

Funny, Tatum couldn't agree more. She might have had her last fat-free frozen yogurt.

The boys were in high spirits. They acted up twice, causing enough of a commotion for customers' heads to swivel in their direction. Tatum cautioned them the first time, using her no-nonsense teacher voice. The boys promptly behaved. For two minutes. A second warning yielded no results.

"That's enough, you two," Ryder scolded.

They immediately quieted. Then, giggling, continued to lick their dripping ice cream. For the moment, peace ensued.

"I'm impressed," Tatum said.

"I'm louder than you."

She wasn't sure about that. Ryder had a way with children. Not just playing with them and being their pal. They also respected him and listened to him.

His former marriage may have been years ago and ended unhappily, but parenting his ex's two daughters, even for a short time, had taught him a lot and allowed his natural tendencies to flourish.

All at once, his cell phone rang. He removed the phone from his pocket and studied the screen, his brows drawing together. Naturally, her curiosity was piqued.

After a moment, he said, "Excuse me," and answered the call.

"No problem." She waved off his concern, then promptly strained to hear his side of the conversation over the din.

"Hi, Myra. Don't tell me, you're working on a Saturday. No, I'm not busy. It's all right." Each sentence was separated by a pause. "Really. Huh. Just a second." He rose from the table and said to Tatum, "Be right back," before stepping away.

Now, her curiosity was more than piqued. It was fired.

"Absolutely." Ryder started for the door, only to be cut off and delayed by a large group of high school students entering the parlor. "I can make it. Nine a.m. sharp. Yeah, I have heard of them. Right. What's the starting salary?"

Starting salary?

"How soon are they looking for someone?" Ryder continued.

Looking for someone? He was talking to this Myra person about a job. He wasn't wasting a moment.

Tatum suffered a sudden emptiness inside.

Finally, Ryder was able to move on and step outside. A few minutes later, he ended the phone call and returned to their table. Even if she hadn't overheard part of his conversation, she'd have guessed that something was up by his guilty expression.

"Sorry about that," he said.

Right. She was the one sorry. His family would be devastated. And, she couldn't tell them. Not without admitting she'd eavesdropped.

"It's all right." She grabbed some napkins from the dispenser and started cleaning up the boys' mess. "We should go. My break is about over."

Drew's "Aw, Mom," was followed by Benjie's "Do we have to?"

"Class starts in five minutes." Tatum was rarely late.

She and Ryder spoke little on the way back.

At the door, they paused. "Looks like the horse's owner came and got him," Ryder said.

Tatum had forgotten all about the runaway.

"Thought for a minute I was going to have to call animal control."

Another pause ensued.

"Thanks for the ice cream," she said. Somehow the thrill of her decadent treat had worn off.

"I'd like to see you later."

Her heart gave a little trill. Was he asking her out? She instantly tamped down the feeling. With an upcoming job interview, probably the first of several, he wouldn't be here much longer.

"To talk," he said.

Oh. About the call she'd overheard. "It isn't necessary."

"Tatum." He reached for her, his hand settling on her waist.

She raised her gaze to his, and her breath caught. He was close enough to…

"Mom!"

At the sound of Gretchen's voice, Tatum spun. There stood her mother-in-law with a sour look on her face, a flailing Adam in her arms, Gretchen at her side.

Just when Tatum thought things couldn't get worse, Adam yelled, "Daddy, Daddy."

Like that, the look on her mother-in-law's face went from sour to infuriated.

Chapter Eight

Ryder bent over Tatum's desk, his hands braced on the edge. She wasn't escaping this time. "You've been avoiding me all week."

"That's not true." She refused to look at him and instead busied herself with a stack of envelopes. "It's only Thursday."

He glanced at the partially open door leading to his mother's office, which was, fortunately, empty. He and Tatum were alone.

"Is it because Adam called me Daddy again?"

She visibly tensed.

"What did she say?" Ryder didn't specify who. Tatum knew he referred to her former mother-in-law.

"Nothing."

"I don't believe you."

"Excuse me." She pushed back from her desk, the wheels on her chair squeaking. "I have to get to the mailbox before noon."

"Tatum, I'm sorry."

She closed her eyes and sighed wistfully. "It's not your fault."

"No, it's Monty's fault. If he visited more often, his son wouldn't be calling me Daddy. The guy's a piece of work if you ask me."

"Adam's just two. He's easily confused."

"My point exactly." Ryder straightened. "What's with

Monty, anyway? Even when my father was a drunk, he always loved his children and spent time with us."

"He wanted you and your sister and would have wanted Liberty if your mother had been honest with him. Monty wasn't ready for a family."

"That's no excuse," he said.

"I need to be careful. Not give Ruth any more ammunition to use against me."

"Ammunition? What? You're not allowed to date? I'm no attorney, but I'm pretty sure Monty and Ruth can't take your kids away from you because you have a boyfriend."

"You're not my boyfriend," Tatum said hotly.

Okay, he deserved that. He'd led her on not once but twice.

"You're legitimately worried about your mother-in-law interfering in your life. I didn't mean to make light of it. But Monty's the one she should be mad at for his complete lack of parental involvement."

"I don't disagree." Tatum's shoulders slumped, her bluster waning. "That's not the reason I've been avoiding you."

"So, you admit it, then."

She looked around as if concerned they were being overheard. "You put me in an awkward position. How am I supposed to stand by and say nothing to your family while you're out there looking for a new job?"

"I apologize again. I shouldn't have talked to that headhunter in front of you."

Grabbing the envelopes, she huffed in frustration and stood.

"What?"

"Honestly, Ryder, you are really dense sometimes."

He'd have laughed if she wasn't so serious. "You'll get no argument from me."

"I'm not the one you should be talking to about this."

She started for the door. "Grab the phone if it rings, will you? I'm going to the mailbox."

"All right." He hated that she was right. "I'll do it."

She paused, her hand on the doorknob. "Do what?"

"You're going to make me say it, aren't you?"

Her eyes narrowed, and she shifted her weight. Ryder had a pretty good idea what it felt like to be a student in her class who'd been caught breaking the rules.

"I'll tell my family I'm actively looking for a new job," he stated flatly.

Tatum's hand fell away from the door. "I feel sorry for them."

"Don't waste your energies just yet."

"Interview the other day not go well?"

He could lie but didn't. "The company wasn't as good a fit as I first thought."

"Oh, well." At least she didn't look smug.

"I want you to come with me."

"Where?"

"I have a meeting with Marshall Whitmen in thirty minutes at the Flat Iron for lunch."

"The head of the Scottsdale Parada del Sol Rodeo?"

"One and the same."

That got a reaction from her. The Parada del Sol was one of Arizona's most prestigious and popular rodeos. Ryder's family had been trying to land the account for years.

"How did that...who set up the meeting?" she asked.

"My father has connections. He heard the bucking stock contractor supplying the horses has pulled out. The distemper virus going around has infected his entire herd."

"That's terrible. But the rodeo is months away. Won't the horses recover by then?"

"Marshall doesn't want to take any chances the bucking stock won't be in top form."

"What possible help can I be at the meeting?"

"It would be a great opportunity for you to see how the negotiations work firsthand."

"Your father and his connections are what got the meeting. He should go with you."

"One of the bulls is acting sick. He's meeting the veterinarian at noon."

Tatum accepted that answer without question. Like everyone at the arena, she was well aware of his father's devotion to the bulls and belief they were the future of the Easy Money.

"Come with me, Tatum," Ryder repeated.

"Because you want someone to take over the marketing and promotion part of your job when you leave."

"Because it will give you the chance to grow your present job skills and increase your earning potential."

"In case the school doesn't hire me back."

"Consider it hedging your bets."

After a lingering hesitation, she smiled. A small, soft one that sent Ryder's pulse soaring. Proof positive she could affect him like none other. He'd promised her he wouldn't compromise her again with touching and kissing. It might be a promise impossible to keep.

She shook her head. "I can't leave the office unattended."

"Let's call my sisters. One of them should be free."

"It's their lunch hour. And they have classes later."

"You're fabricating excuses."

"Not exactly—"

The office door abruptly opened and Ryder's mother entered. She took one look at Tatum and Ryder, then stopped in her tracks. "What's going on?"

"Ryder's…" Tatum faltered.

"I'm trying to convince her to come with me to meet with Marshall Whitmen." He waited for his mother's objection, only she surprised him.

"I think that's a great idea!"

"The phones," Tatum objected.

"I'll watch them."

Ryder allowed himself a huge grin. Round one had gone to him.

"YOUR MOTHER HAS an ulterior motive." Tatum sent Ryder an arch look.

"Do tell."

The Flat Iron Restaurant was ten minutes from the arena. Ryder had stretched the drive into fifteen—on purpose, she was convinced. Mostly, he'd talked about Marshall Whitmen and his take on how the meeting would progress. Now that they were nearing the restaurant, she had only a minute at most to speak her mind.

"She's matchmaking."

"You think?" he teased.

"Be serious, Ryder."

"Why would she?"

"She saw us kissing the other night."

He took his time responding. "She told you?"

For a moment, Tatum relived that embarrassing moment. "It's no fun chitchatting with your boss about kissing her son."

"Sorry. I asked her not to."

"You knew she saw us and didn't tell me?" Tatum ground her teeth together in frustration. "A little warning would have been nice."

"She's making something out of nothing."

His observation, delivered nonchalantly, shouldn't have bothered Tatum. She, as much as he, had put the brakes on any potential romance between them. Yet, she was bothered.

"Don't you get it?" Tatum had accused Ryder of being dense earlier, partially in jest. Now, she was less sure. "Your mother is willing to orchestrate a romance between us if it encourages you to stay."

"What if she is? What's the harm? Nothing will come of it."

That word again. Nothing.

Tatum silently fumed. Her anger didn't last, and she put on her best smile. Ryder's reminder that they had no future together was no reason to ruin this very important meeting.

He opened the front door of the restaurant for her, and she preceded him inside. All around them, the restaurant clanked, clattered and bustled with activity. Delicious aromas filled the air. A chalkboard on the wall advertised the day's specials.

Ryder hitched his chin in the direction of a booth. "Marshall's already here."

At his possessive and unexpected grip on her arm, she drew in a sharp breath. Before she could speak, he propelled her ahead of him, his fingers gliding along the inside of her forearm before he released her.

"This way."

She blinked, momentarily disoriented by the delicious sensation his touch evoked.

Marshall Whitmen tossed down his napkin and rose at their approach. He must have been quite early for he'd already ordered an iced tea. His welcoming smile assured Tatum that he didn't object to her presence.

"Good day, Ryder." He tipped his cowboy hat at her. "And who's your lovely companion?"

Hands were shaken. Marshall's grip on hers was strong and that of a man thirty years younger. With his white hair and matching white beard, he could have passed for Colonel Sanders's brother.

"This is Tatum Mayweather," Ryder said. "She's the arena's office manager and has been showing me the ropes. I hope you don't mind that she came along."

A blatant exaggeration. If anything, the complete opposite was true. Ryder was showing *her* the ropes. But she followed his lead, understanding without being told that these types of meetings were a game with established plays.

"Not at all." Marshall's tone dripped honey. "A lovely woman enhances any meal. Even better when she's smart and talented."

Oh, he was a charmer all right. Smooth as silk. Nonetheless, Tatum felt herself soften. "I've admired your work with the Parada del Sol for years," she said. "You have a stellar reputation." He was also well-liked and considered to be fair and honest.

Ryder sent her an approving look. Tatum warmed. She wanted to help the Becketts for all the favors they'd done her. More than that, she wanted to please Ryder and not give him cause to regret his decision to bring her along.

"Do you mind if I take notes?" she asked and withdrew her ever-present spiral notebook from her purse. It was filled with grocery lists, appointment reminders and Gretchen's doodles. But Ryder and Marshall didn't need to know that.

"Good idea." Marshall beamed. "These days I can't trust this old memory of mine."

Ryder motioned for her to slide into the booth. She scooted all the way to the wall to make room for him. Still, it was cramped. Bumping body parts was inevitable—and distracting.

They didn't talk business until their lunch orders were placed. Ryder, Tatum noticed, waited, taking his lead from Marshall. Once the subject was broached, he pitched the Easy Money's bucking stock with the confidence of someone who'd been a member of the family business his entire life.

"You know the quality of our horses, Marshall. There are none better in Arizona."

"Absolutely. Wouldn't be here today if I didn't."

"Every one of our head has been vet-checked this past week. No signs of distemper. We'll continue our diligence up until the rodeo and provide health certificates upon delivery of the stock, dated no later than one day before the rodeo. That's a guarantee."

Marshall nodded thoughtfully. "Sounds fair."

Negotiations ceased when the food arrived. Evidently, Marshall didn't conduct business while eating. The men started on their burgers. Tatum resisted devouring her salad. Eating out was a real treat for her. It beat her brown bag lunch any day of the week.

"I know a Mayweather," Marshall said to Tatum. "Monty Mayweather. Former bull rider. Any relation to you?"

"My ex-husband."

"Apologies if I brought up a sore subject."

"None needed. Monty and I are on good terms." Interesting how the slight fib slipped easily off her tongue. This wasn't the place or time to admit her lousy ex-husband cared more about his freedom than his three children.

"His loss." Marshall sent Ryder a look that, if Tatum interpreted it correctly, meant Ryder's gain.

"Tatum's also an art instructor. She has a studio in town."

She wanted to kick Ryder under the table. Why had he brought that up?

"Do tell." Marshall studied her with interest. "I dabble a bit with oils myself."

"Really?" Now it was her turn to show interest.

"A hobby. Mostly."

"Some of Marshall's paintings are hanging in the lobby at the Scottsdale Civic Center." Ryder angled his head away from the rodeo promoter and winked at Tatum.

She felt foolish. There had been a reason for him to mention her studio. She and Marshall shared a love of art.

"That's wonderful," she said with heartfelt enthusiasm. "You must be very talented."

He shrugged off the compliment. "I wouldn't say that.

My wife, being a member of the chamber of commerce for twenty-plus years, might have more to do with it."

Talk turned to the upcoming Wild West Days. The waitress had hardly removed their empty plates when Ryder said, "We'd love to have you and your family as our guests at the rodeo finals on Sunday afternoon."

"Why, thank you. It's much appreciated."

Tatum picked up her pad and pen. "I'll have passes delivered to your office tomorrow. VIP section." She didn't ask Ryder's permission before making the offer, confident he wouldn't object. "Is four enough? Or six?"

"Four's plenty. Leena and I will bring the grandkids."

"Looking forward to meeting them." Ryder confidently eased into the rest of his pitch. "That'll give you a chance to observe our bucking stock up close."

"The Lost Dutchman has also approached me."

Ryder nodded. "Donnie's stock is top-notch."

"It must be, or you wouldn't use him yourself."

"For bulls," Ryder was quick to clarify. "For now."

"You buying more?"

"My father's in the process."

The waitress returned and refilled their iced tea glasses. Talk continued, eventually getting down to the nitty-gritty. Tatum's pen made scratching noises as she jotted down numbers and dates and dollar amounts. Working for the Becketts, she'd typed, revised and filed enough contracts to know these terms were good, each party giving up something but getting something better in return.

Ryder demonstrated a real knack for negotiating, impressing Tatum. If he stayed in Reckless, he could do a lot to take the Easy Money to the next level. Like his father had back in the days before he started drinking. Then again, Ryder's talents were perhaps wasted in a small town. He was used to greater challenges and a faster-paced environment.

"As much as I enjoyed this, I have to get back to the office." Marshall reached for the hat he'd set on the seat beside him. "Write up a letter of intent and email it to me. We'll go from there."

"I'll have it for you tomorrow." Ryder tossed several bills on to the table for a tip.

He'd also picked up the lunch tab. It was Tatum's guess Marshall was frequently treated to meals by bucking stock contractors vying for his business. Even so, he'd thanked Ryder graciously.

"I'm looking forward to working with you," Ryder said at the door. They'd stopped just outside the restaurant before parting ways.

"Tell your parents hello for me." Marshall adjusted his hat, pushing down on the crown. "Have to say, I was a little surprised to hear Mercer had returned to the Beckett fold. Your mama was dead set against him for years."

"You aren't the only one surprised."

"Then again, you've returned, too."

Ryder grinned pleasantly. "Things change."

"That, they do." Marshall gave a small wave as he strolled away. "Including the outfits that supply bucking stock for the Parada del Sol."

Excitement coursed through Tatum. The signatures had yet to be signed on the dotted line, but it appeared the Becketts had just landed a lucrative new client. She was thrilled to have contributed in her small way.

"Nicely done," she said to Ryder when they were alone.

"I like Marshall. He made it easy."

"There's nothing easy about negotiating a contract."

"Beats pleading with store owners to put our posters in their windows." He showered her with a breathtaking smile. "You were good. I think you should attend every meeting."

She laughed as they crossed the parking lot to his truck. The sun beat down on them, unusually warm for late September. In the distance, the mountains shimmered, their foliage more brown than green this time of year.

"Sure," she said. "But only when the client also happens to be an artist."

"First rule of any sales meeting. Find common ground and make a connection."

"I think the free passes were more of an inducement than the fact Marshall and I both like to paint."

Ryder shook his head. "Free passes were just added insurance."

The truck was hot when they climbed in, and the leather seat burned the backs of Tatum's legs even through the fabric of her slacks. "Why are you doing this, Ryder?" She fastened her seat belt. "And don't tell me it's because you could be leaving."

He inserted his key and started the engine. The truck, a one-ton diesel, roared to life. "You're smart and talented and capable of doing more than managing an office."

"Right. And you don't feel the least bit guilty about my former mother-in-law giving me grief because Adam called you Daddy."

"I'm not that noble, Tatum. Though, I'd like you to think that if it raises your opinion of me."

"Quit joking."

He drove for several more minutes before answering. "When I picked up Benjie the other day at the studio, Lenny Faust mentioned being on the school board with my mother."

"Yes." She let the single syllable word trail.

"He didn't sound optimistic about the board voting in the new budget."

"Ryder, I—"

He cut her off. "It's like the passes we're giving Marshall. You learning to negotiate contracts is added insurance. Make yourself indispensable to my parents, Tatum."

She chewed on that for a moment. With more to contribute, she'd feel less like a charity case. And if she had any chance of affording a larger place to rent, one that met with her mother-in-law's approval, she'd need to boost her income. If she didn't get her old teaching job back, elevating her earning potential at the arena might be her only solution.

To accomplish that, Ryder would have to leave town and vacate his job. That would devastate his family.

It would also, she realized, devastate her.

Chapter Nine

Only one night remained before the start of the Wild West Days Rodeo. Fridays were traditionally the first round of competition and always important. Points earned went a long way toward participants qualifying for the final round on Sunday.

Which meant Thursday evening was the last chance for riders to practice. The Easy Money parking area was packed with vehicles and trailers. The stands held family and friends, there to support and encourage. Every available pen was teeming with activity. Every available hand toiled laboriously. Ryder's family scurried around like the proverbial chickens with their heads cut off. Ryder included.

The livestock, however, rested. They had a lot of work ahead of them and needed to be in tip-top shape. The Lost Dutchman bulls had arrived that morning, fit and full of themselves. Mercer had spent the day inspecting each one from horns to tail, pronouncing them raring to go.

In lieu of calves, ropers were using a Heel-O-Matic to hone their skills. The mechanical device consisted of a heavy-duty fake calf mounted on to a three-wheeled dolly. Tonight, the dolly was pulled by one of the wranglers driving an ATV. Cowboys exploded from behind the barrier and, if their aim was true, roped the head of the fake calf. It didn't exactly mimic the real thing, but it came close enough.

The barrel racers had finished thirty minutes ago, after

an intense two-hour practice session, and turned the arena over to the ropers. Bull and bronc riders, if they weren't competing in other events, took the night off and, like the bulls and horses, rested up for tomorrow.

"On deck, Ryder," Cassidy called. She stood near the box, calling off the names of cowboys in the order they'd signed up.

What in the world had possessed Ryder to think he could rope after all these years? Even a fake calf attached to a three-wheeled dolly exceeded his abilities.

The idea had come to him an hour ago. When Tatum and her family arrived, to be specific. She'd taken the kids to the pizza parlor in town for dinner, then returned to the arena to assist if needed. Mostly, they were watching the ropers practice.

Drew, so Ryder had been told, was going a little stir-crazy at the day care, what with not being able to play outside because of his cast. Tatum had thought spending an evening with Ryder's nephew, Benjie, would take some of the edge off. Benjie was doing his best to corrupt Drew and entice him into playing when he should be sitting quietly.

Ryder sympathized. He felt a little stir-crazy himself, which could explain his present circumstances.

He and his mother were talking, but only when they couldn't avoid it. Cassidy blamed him for upsetting their mother and had let him know in no uncertain terms. Mercer had gotten wind of his job interview—Ryder's fault for leaving his contract with Myra on his dresser. As a result, his father and Liberty were constantly needling Ryder to stay. Then, there was Tatum. To protect them both, he was maintaining a strictly professional relationship with her.

That didn't stop him from wanting to pull her in his arms every time he got within ten feet of her. And those wounded expressions she continually wore made it all the harder.

Tightening his grip on the lariat hanging by his side, he forced himself to relax. He'd wanted Tatum to see he could still compete with the best of them despite years of working in an office. Instead, he was about to humiliate himself.

"Let's go, Ryder," Cassidy called, then spoke into a handheld radio. She'd been giving instructions to the young man driving the ATV since practice started. He reversed direction and lined up the Heel-O-Matic, backing the fake calf into place.

Ryder jogged his horse to the box and got in position. This wasn't his first outing on the young gelding. Twice he'd gone for a short ride, the last time with Liberty. He'd also found a spare hour to throw a few tosses with a lariat. The hay bale he'd used for a target didn't lope across the arena like a live calf or bump along like the Heel-O-Matic.

Something told him he'd need a lot more practice riding and roping if he expected to impress Tatum.

When he was ready, one hand gripping the reins, the other on his lariat, he nodded to his sister and said, "Go."

She signaled the young man driving the ATV. At once, Ryder and the fake calf were off and running.

The gelding responded immediately and perfectly to Ryder's cues, going from a standstill to a full gallop in the blink of an eye. Ryder's hat flew off, but he didn't pay attention.

Instincts he'd been certain were gone for good suddenly kicked in, and he let them guide him. Arm in the air, high over his head, he twirled the rope. As the gelding thundered across the arena floor in pursuit of the fake calf, Ryder took aim and let the rope fly.

He watched it stretch out in front him, steady and true. Elation filled him. God, he'd missed this. The thrill. The rush. The excitement. He may not have made rodeoing his career, but there was no reason he couldn't make a hobby of it. Especially if he stayed in Reckless.

And, just like that, the noose missed the fake calf's head by a good foot. The rope fell to the ground, limp and lifeless as a cut clothesline. The gelding, sensing there would be no battle with the calf, slowed to a trot before coming to an abrupt halt and snorting—in disgust, Ryder thought.

"That makes two of us, boy." He patted the gelding's neck.

One of the wranglers ran over and returned Ryder's hat. "Good try, partner."

Ryder thanked him and reeled in his rope, his gaze searching the stands. Great. There was Tatum and the kids. All of them watching. She waved. He raised his hat in response before plunking it down on his head.

He should have known better than to try and show off. What was he? Fifteen again?

Behind the bucking chutes, he dismounted. His ploy to be alone with his shame didn't work.

"Tough luck, son."

At least his father didn't patronize him. "I'm a little rusty."

"The good news is you can always improve."

"Need help with anything?"

His father chuckled. "Looking for an excuse not to embarrass yourself again?"

"Guess those practice sessions behind the barn didn't pay off."

"You picked the right horse, anyway."

"Good thing. He alone saved me from complete humiliation."

Most competitors brought their own riding stock to a rodeo. The Becketts maintained a few head in reserve for cowboys whose horses sustained an injury or suffered an illness that knocked them from the competition. This gelding was one of the reserve stock.

"If you have a minute," his father said, "I want to run an idea by you."

"I'm all ears." Ryder continued walking the horse, letting him cool down. His father fell into step beside him.

"I got a call earlier today. Do you remember Harlo Billings?"

"The stock contractor from Waco?"

"One and the same. He's retiring a month from now and looking to sell his bucking stock."

Ryder didn't need a map to see where this conversation was going. "How many bulls?"

"More than we need or can afford. I have my eye on ten bulls and three championship producing heifers. Two of the bulls are high-dollar earners."

"Impressive. But that's a lot of stock for a single purchase."

"He's willing to let them go for a good price."

When his father named the amount, Ryder released a low whistle. "You weren't kidding."

"He's more interested in the bulls finding the right home where they can reach their full potential than making a killer profit."

Ryder debated stating the obvious. The partnership agreement between his parents, written when they'd divorced—and kept secret from their children until recently—didn't allow one of the partners to contribute assets or make purchases without the consent of the other. That clause had caused a heated disagreement when Ryder's father bought the first six bulls.

"What does Mom think of the idea?" he asked.

"I haven't told her yet."

Figured. "Do you even have the money?"

"Enough for a down payment. Harlo's agreed to carry the remaining balance over the next five years at an interest rate better than the banks are offering."

"Very generous of him."

"He knows what these bulls are capable of and their earning potential. It's a safe investment for him."

"You planning a trip to Waco to inspect the bulls?"

"I've seen them. Just this past summer at the Crosby Fair and Rodeo."

"You'll have to convince Mom. Any financial note needs to be signed by the two of you.

"I am. I will." His father sent him a sly grin. "I was hoping you'd be there when I raise the subject."

Ah. To act as a buffer "I should let you face her alone."

"You think I'm afraid?"

Ryder grinned despite himself. "If you're smart, you will be. She's pretty formidable when she's riled."

They reached the barn. Ryder led the gelding down the aisle toward the tack room. While his father watched, he unsaddled and brushed the gelding, then returned him to his stall. His last task was to bring a bucket of oats. The horse would need his energy for the upcoming weekend.

"With that many bulls, we may have to hire a handler," Ryder mused aloud.

"I already have someone in mind. Shane Westcott."

"Don't think I know him."

They strolled to the arena and watched the practice continue.

"Shane's been around a long time," his father said. "Came into his own a couple years after you left the circuit. Retired a champion after walking away from a fall that should have killed him."

"Is he in the market for a job?"

"No. But I'm not letting a little thing like that stop me."

Ryder didn't doubt his father's abilities. With the exception of his mother, Mercer Beckett could sweet-talk *any*one into almost *any*thing. Hadn't he convinced Ryder to return when it was the last thing he wanted?

"You need to buy the bulls and heifers first."

"Timing is everything. I'm going to wait until after Wild West Days to tell your mother."

"Tell her what?"

Both men spun to find Cassidy staring at them, hands

planted on her hips. Ryder was instantly reminded of the day Gretchen had caught him in the stall with Cupcake. He half expected Cassidy to scream for their mother at the top of her lungs.

"Nothing." Their father leaned an arm on the arena fence as if all was right with the world. "Just talking arena business."

"Liar," she spat. "You haven't changed at all. You're still the same deceitful SOB Mom threw out of the house."

Their father jerked as if she'd backhanded him.

"Cassidy." Ryder stepped forward. "That's enough."

"It's okay." Their father pushed off the fence. "She's right. I was lying."

Cassidy pivoted.

Before she could leave, their father hooked her by the arm. "Wait. Honey, please."

"Let go of me."

"I'm considering buying some additional bulls and three heifers."

"You can't. Not without Mom's approval."

"That's what Ryder was saying. And I told him I was waiting until after this weekend. There's no big secret."

"Then why lie to me?" Her eyes sparked with accusation.

"I shouldn't have. I just wanted to avoid a huge fight right before the rodeo."

"Because you know Mom doesn't want to buy any more bulls."

Ryder had thought to let things play out between his father and sister. Her attitude changed his mind. "You can't speak for her, Cassidy. And the fact is, none of us, you, me or Liberty, has any say in the running of the arena."

"I thought this was a family-owned business." She visibly bristled. "Doesn't my opinion count?"

"Nothing's been decided," their father said. "And nothing will be without a family meeting. But I'm going to be honest with you, that won't take place until after I speak to your mother."

Ryder's father wisely omitted the part where he'd asked Ryder to be in on that discussion.

Cassidy stared at them both for several seconds. When she spoke, it was through clenched teeth. "You're only saying that because I overheard you."

"Cassidy." Ryder had had his fill of his sister's dramatics. "You're being unreasonable."

"You always did side with Dad."

"And you've always sided with Mom."

Cassidy opened her mouth to speak. The next instant, she clamped it shut and stormed off. But not before Ryder noticed tears gleaming in her eyes.

"That didn't go exactly as planned," his father said.

The casual remark irked Ryder. "She has a point. You did lie to her, now and in the past."

"Now, wait a damn minute."

"Mom lied, too." Ryder's gaze traveled the entire arena grounds. For one surreal moment, the place looked strange to him. As if he'd never seen it before. "Why am I here? Why do I even bother?"

"What are you talking about?"

"Everyone wants me to reconcile with Mom, but what about you refusing to get along with Cassidy?"

"It isn't that simple."

"None of this is." Ryder didn't care who saw them and vented his anger. "I've always blamed Mom for dividing this family when she threw you out, and lying to you about being Liberty's dad. But you're doing the same thing. Splitting us right down the middle."

"Be patient, son."

"You know something, Dad? I didn't quit my last job. Not unless you count leaving rather than being fired as quitting. And you know why I was going to be fired? Because I screwed up by allowing my personal life to affect

my professional one. From that little display I just witnessed between you and Cassidy, I'd say you're guilty of
the same thing."

He stormed ahead, leaving his father behind.

Come Monday, Ryder would call Myra and do whatever
she advised. Go on interviews. Career coaching. Refresher
classes. Get a new haircut and buy a new suit if the headhunter thought it would make a difference. Anything to get
the hell out of Reckless.

"YOU'RE UNDER ARREST," the sheriff said and aimed his pistol at the bank robber's chest.

"You'll never take me alive." The dirty, ragged man
squirmed in an attempt to break free of the two deputies
pinning his arms.

"This day's been a long time coming, Johnny Waco."

"You might have killed old Lazy Eye Joe, but you ain't
got me yet." All at once, the bank robber broke free and
made a run for it down the center of the street.

The sheriff raised his pistol and fired. Smoke exploded
from the tip of the gun but no bullet. Even so, the bank robber threw up his arms and face-planted in the street, then
writhed melodramatically as if his last breath were leaving
his body. The crowd gasped in shock and fear.

"You got him, Sheriff," one of the deputies said, awe
and respect in his voice.

The sheriff holstered his pistol. "That scum and his
good-for-nothing partner will never bother the decent and
upstanding people of Reckless again."

The crowd broke into applause. As if touched by a magic
wand, Johnny Waco and his partner, Lazy Eye Joe, sprang
to their feet, fully restored. The second deputy, a teenager
no older than Ryder had been when he'd performed in the
Wild West Days shoot-outs, distributed flyers.

"Next show's at one o'clock," the sheriff announced.
"Then at three and five. Deputy Maynard here is handing

out the schedule." The sheriff wagged a warning finger. "Remember, you ne'er do wells and troublemakers. At any time, any place, you could be apprehended. Criminals will be thrown in jail. And for you men taking advantage of our lovely, innocent ladies, pay special heed. There's been more than one shotgun wedding in these parts." He winked. "All fines and fees will be donated to the local public library. So, if you are apprehended, be generous."

Lively conversation erupted around Ryder while residents of Reckless, and tourists settled in for the parade, due to start shortly.

He'd left the lineup on the north side of town where he'd been helping his family ready the Easy Money Vaqueros. The arena's students were the tenth entry in the parade. His parents were riding along with the students, as well as Cassidy and her son Benjie.

Liberty and her fiancé, Deacon, would be watching from the sidelines. Ryder had left in search of Tatum and her children, hoping to join them.

No sense making excuses, he'd decided. At least to himself. He wanted to see her. She was the safe harbor in a storm, and he'd been in the midst of an emotional hurricane since Thursday evening when he'd argued with Cassidy and their father. Luckily, he supposed, they'd all been busy with the rodeo and hadn't talked much to each other. When they did, it was all business.

The sidewalks were packed. Every few feet, Ryder bumped into someone and offered an apology. People had made miniature camps in front of storefronts, using folding chairs, stools and even ice chests as seats. Food vendors, in their trucks and carts, were stationed at every corner, reminding Ryder that it had been years since he'd last eaten a corn dog or fry bread.

He had no idea where Tatum was; they, too, hadn't spoken since yesterday. Was she frustrated with the latest Beckett squabble and letting him know?

Instinct guided him in the direction of the Ship-With-Ease Store and her art studio. A few minutes later, his guess paid off. She perched on a lawn chair with Adam in her lap. Beside her, Gretchen and Drew moved their matching child-size lawn chairs into place.

Pleasure brought a smile to his face and a spring to his step. The next instant, he came to a grinding halt, and his spirits sank. Her former mother-in-law, Ruth, sat beside the kids and looked decidedly displeased to see him.

Bad timing. The worst. Tatum must have invited her to the parade, since it wasn't her usual day to visit.

Before he could turn around and leave, Tatum glanced in his direction. His name issued softly from her lips. "Ryder."

Escape became impossible when Drew looked over and spotted him. "Mr. Beckett!" The next instant, the boy was out of his chair and running.

"Drew," Tatum called. "Come back."

Ryder's legs took the brunt of Drew's impact. "Hey, buddy. How you doing?"

Holding on to Ryder's waist, he stared up with huge eyes. "Will you watch the parade with us?"

"I'm not sure…"

"Daddy!" Arms waving, Adam struggled to free himself from Tatum's grasp.

"Adam, that's not your father," Tatum said but not fast enough.

"Haven't you corrected him yet?" Ruth asked icily.

"Several times." Tatum tried to restrain Adam. "He hasn't caught on."

"If Daddy was here," Gretchen said, "Adam wouldn't be confused."

Everyone stared at her. From the mouths of babes, Ryder thought.

"That's enough from you, young lady," her grandmother scolded.

Gretchen's bottom lip began to tremble.

"It's all right, sweet pea," Tatum soothed and opened her free arm.

The girl jumped from her chair in order to snuggle with her mother.

"I'll catch up with you later." Ryder touched the brim of his cowboy hat and addressed the older woman. "Ma'am."

"No!"

Tatum's outburst halted him.

"Please," she implored. "Join us."

He understood then. She didn't want to be alone with her mother-in-law. And while he normally avoided other people's family drama—he had plenty of his own—he stayed. Because Tatum had asked.

"You can have my seat," Drew offered.

"I think it might be a bit too small for me. I'll stand."

"Here." The elderly gentleman next to them pushed a plastic crate over.

"If you're sure."

"We're not using it."

"Thank you." Ryder placed the crate next to Tatum's chair and sat. Leaning forward, he peered around her. "Nice to see you again, Mrs. Mayweather. Hope you're enjoying Wild West Days."

"I am. Thank you." Her mouth barely moved when she talked.

Okay, Ryder admitted it. He was purposely trying to push her buttons.

"We saw the shoot-out." Drew squeezed himself between Ryder's knees.

Adam squealed and doubled his efforts to get down. "Daddy! Wanna see Daddy."

"Here." Mrs. Mayweather reached across the two small folding chairs. "I'll take him," she insisted.

Adam wasn't happy being denied, and Tatum made her point by taking her ever-loving time relinquishing her son to his grandmother.

Good for you, Ryder thought.

Gretchen stole the spot in her mother's lap that her baby brother had vacated. They were still sitting that way, the two children's chairs empty, when the sound of clip-clopping hooves signaled the start of the parade.

The mayor and grand marshal came first, seated atop a replica stagecoach drawn by four horses. A pair of colorfully dressed clowns came after the stagecoach. Carrying scoop shovels, they were accompanied by a third clown pushing a wheelbarrow. The trio joked with the crowd, pantomiming for laughs. Their real job was to clean up any "accidents" the horses might have, clearing the way for the next entrant.

After the clowns came the grade-school marching band and the Future Farmers of America. Their float, a flatbed trailer covered with streamers, was pulled by a tractor. The marina also had an entry—a boat on wheels—as did the mining company.

"That reminds me." Tatum leaned close to Ryder. "I heard back from the mining company secretary yesterday. Sorry I forgot to tell you."

"And?"

"She sounded interested. Said she'd give us a call at the end of January."

Three months away. "That's something, I suppose."

"I mentioned our ability to accommodate team-building activities."

"Can we do that?"

"We could by the end of January."

Ryder grinned, glad their former camaraderie had returned. "Always thinking, Tatum. I like that."

"I can't take all the credit. We practice team-building exercises in school."

They continued watching the parade, periodically conversing over the children's chatter. The Easy Money Vaqueros earned a loud round of applause from the spectators.

When the Shriners passed by, throwing candy and small trinkets onto the sidewalks, children fell on the prizes like starving dogs with a bone.

"I had some upsetting news yesterday," Tatum said. "Lenny's considering renting my space out at the first of the year."

That took Ryder aback. "Why?'

"He got a notice from his landlord. His lease is coming up for renewal, and they want to raise the rent."

"What about your classes?"

"It won't matter if I get my teaching job back."

"I thought you wanted to keep up the art classes even if you did."

"No. Yes." She gave a one-shoulder shrug. "I have this sort of crazy idea. A new career if the school doesn't re-hire me."

"Tell me."

"It's stupid, really. I don't have the money needed to start a business."

Ryder was intrigued. "What kind of business?"

She glanced quickly at Ruth, who was preoccupied with her grandchildren. Tatum spoke in a hushed voice. "A craft store. I'd also stock art and teaching supplies, so my teacher friends wouldn't have to drive into Globe." She smiled. "Of course, I'd devote an entire section of the store to my art classes."

"I think it's a great idea."

"Be serious." She blushed prettily. "A craft store in Reckless? Arizona's most Western town?"

"All right, I admit to being supportive of any new busi-ness venture. But what you've described makes sense. The people in this town have a need, and you've developed a business to fill it. Plus, it's something you'd be good at."

"Now, if I could just win the lottery."

"Get a small business loan."

"Let's be honest." She sighed. "My credit history isn't the best."

She was talking about losing her house. "There were mitigating circumstances. What counts is that you got yourself back on your feet. And quickly, too."

"Not sure I'm fully back on my feet yet."

"I could help you. I happen to be good at managing money." Ryder had spent most of his professional career developing budgets for clients and working within those budgets.

"If you're still here. Cassidy mentioned you took off yesterday morning, and were gone for a few hours."

Evidently his second consultation with Myra hadn't gone unnoticed. "Did she tell you we argued?"

"The way she put it, she argued with your father, and you got involved."

"Frankly, it was a free-for-all. Dad and I had words, too, after she left."

"I'm sorry."

Ryder reassured himself that Ruth was still not listening before confessing, "I did meet with the headhunter."

Tatum gave him an I-told-you-so look. Because he couldn't think of a comeback, he said nothing.

They watched the remaining parade in relative silence, commenting now and then on something of interest. Thirty minutes later, the parade came to an end. Almost immediately, the crowd began to disperse. Ryder thought the time had come for him to take his leave.

"See you at the rodeo tonight."

"Don't go," Drew whined and hurried over.

Tatum didn't second her son's plea. If her mother-in-law wasn't there, he'd question her. Was she mad because he might leave Reckless still at odds with his family or mad because he might leave her?

"Thanks for the use of the crate." Ryder pushed it toward the elderly gentleman. When he straightened, he found himself face-to-face with Tatum. She'd been tying Drew's shoelace.

For a long moment, they simply stared at each other.

"What's going on?" her mother-in-law asked.

Ryder and Tatum instantly sprang apart.

Drew just couldn't keep quiet. "Mom and Mr. Beckett like each other," he singsonged.

Tatum inhaled sharply. "Drew!"

Before Ryder could offer an explanation, he was grabbed from behind, his arms anchored by the strong grip of one of the deputies.

"Just come with me, sir. If you know what's good for you."

"Wait a minute," Ryder protested.

"It'll go easier for you if you don't make a fuss. This young lady's father insists you do right by her."

"What?" Ryder twisted to see over his shoulder. Another deputy had a hold of Tatum.

"This way, sir."

"My father's in Michigan." Tatum's objection also fell on deaf ears.

The two of them were escorted across the street to the judge's stand in front of the library.

Donnie Statler sat behind the table, wearing a black judge's robe and spectacles. "You're in a lot of trouble, young man."

"How much do I owe, your honor?" Ryder was more than happy to make a donation.

"Not so fast. We're far from done here."

Ryder turned to Tatum, his brows raised.

She shook her head in bewilderment.

Donnie banged his gavel. "I need two volunteers to witness the union between this man and this woman."

Chapter Ten

Tatum didn't know who was responsible for this…this…
stunt—she'd put her money on Sunny—but when she found
out, they were going to get a very large piece of her mind.
Forced into a mock wedding ceremony with Ryder! Of all
the nerve. Thank goodness her mother-in-law had been
nearby and able to watch the kids.

Her mother-in-law! Oh, my God. What must she be
thinking? She already didn't like Ryder just because Adam
called him Daddy. Which he wouldn't do if he saw more
of Monty.

Could her day get any worse?

Even though the young deputy holding her was bigger
and stronger, she tried wrenching free. He held fast.

"Now, now. Your pa will have my hide if I let you get
away."

"My pa!" she sputtered and whirled on him, then gasped
with shock. Her eyes narrowed. "I know you."

He averted his head.

"You're Kenny's cousin." Kenny was a teenager who
worked part-time at the arena.

No doubt remained. Sunny had to be behind this. Damn
her blasted matchmaking scheme.

"First order of business," the judge continued in a booming voice, "is the marriage license fee. Customary amount
is ten dollars but we'll gladly accept more. And my clerk
over there takes credit cards." He motioned to a young
woman with a scanner attached to her smart phone.

My, how times had changed.

Ryder, also closely guarded by a deputy, reached into his back pocket and withdrew his wallet.

"You don't have to do that," Tatum said.

Ryder spared her a sideways glance, then withdrew two twenties. Quadruple the fee. Well, that was nice of him, and the amount would buy a lot of books for the library.

Her earlier irritation toward him evaporated. He really was a generous guy. All he'd done was offer to help her with a craft store business that would likely never see the light of day, and all she'd done was chastise him, then practically ignore him.

"Let's get this over with," he grumbled.

She immediately retracted all her good and kind thoughts about him and snapped, "You aren't the only one being put on the spot."

"Shall we proceed with the vows?" The judge indicated the man guarding Ryder. "Do you have the rings, Deputy?"

The man fished two items from his shirt front pocket. "Right here, your honor." He gave one to Ryder and the other to Tatum.

She reluctantly accepted the dime store plastic ring. Green? Really? Who had a green wedding ring? Ryder's, she noticed, was blue.

"Do you, Tatum Mayweather, take Ryder Beckett as your lawfully wedded husband? To have and to hold until death do you part?"

She rolled her eyes.

"Hurry up, miss." The judge glared at her. "Yours isn't the only ceremony I have scheduled today."

In that moment, she recognized him. Donnie Statler from the Lost Dutchman Rodeo Company and a friend of the Becketts. The robe and slicked-back hair had thrown her off. Sunny was certainly calling in the favors.

"Fine." Tatum ground out.

"I believe the correct response is, I do."

"Okay. I do." She caught sight of Ryder, and her breath abruptly stilled. He didn't look nearly as perturbed as she felt.

"Your turn," the judge—make that, Donnie—said to Ryder. "Do you, Ryder Beckett, take Tatum Mayweather as your lawfully wedded wife? To have and to hold until death do you part?"

Ryder didn't hesitate. He captured both of Tatum's hands in his and gazed deeply into her eyes. "I do."

He did? He would? Her knees weakened even as her heart beat wildly with the anticipation of a bride on her wedding day.

Wait, wait, wait. This wasn't real. She and Ryder weren't getting married. And, yet, a part of her, the part that held her true feelings for him in a small, secret place, wanted to believe it.

"Now for the rings," Donnie said. "Tatum, repeat after me. With this ring, I thee wed."

She heard the pretend judge through a haze and, despite her impaired senses, repeated the words. With trembling fingers, she placed the green ring on Ryder's finger. It slid easily over his knuckle, fitting as if custom-made. She stared at the ring for several seconds, mesmerized.

Taking her hand, Ryder slipped the blue ring onto her left finger. It, too, fit perfectly. "With this ring, I thee wed."

Tears stung Tatum's eyes. She couldn't be crying. Not here, not now. Blinking, she fought to bring her spiraling emotions under control.

Donnie banged his gavel again, giving her a start. "I now pronounce you man and wife. Young man, you may kiss your bride."

A kiss! She'd forgotten about that part.

Tatum had no time to prepare herself before Ryder's mouth claimed hers with a possessiveness that was every bit as wonderful as she might have wished for.

He didn't break away, even when one of the deputies

cleared his throat. Neither did she. His arms, firm and strong, circled her waist and drew her closer. Tatum had no choice but to go up on her tiptoes.

Actually, technically, she did have another option. But she wasn't about to end this incredible, impossible moment.

"Setting the bar kind of high for the rest of us, aren't you?" The remark came from a man in the audience.

Audience! She'd somehow forgotten they weren't alone. Quickly, she pulled away. When Ryder didn't stop her, she scrambled down the platform steps and plunged into the crowd.

Where were her children? Her glance darted from one end of the street to the other. Back at the store? They must be.

She hadn't gone far when Ryder caught up with her. "Wait."

"Please. Not now."

He kept up with her frantic scurrying. "I'm sorry," he said. "I took things too far."

"It wasn't your fault." She'd participated fully. Willingly. "I think your mother set us up." She scanned nearby faces, furtively searching for those of her children.

"She may have. But the kiss was my idea and mine alone."

"Ryder, it's okay."

"I won't bother you again."

"Bother?" She stopped short.

"Bad choice of words," he said.

"No kidding."

Knocking back his cowboy hat, he chuckled dryly. "How is it I can never say or do the right thing around you?"

"And that's funny?" She reached for her purse, only to realize she'd left it behind on her lawn chair. So much for phoning her mother-in-law.

"That was a self-deprecating laugh."

"Mommy!" Gretchen's cry carried over the crowd. "We're here."

Relief flooded Tatum. She started forward, only to have Ryder block her path.

"I have an appointment early next week in Globe with a potential new client. I want you to come along and shadow me."

"No."

"We're a good team. We proved that with Marshall Whitmen."

"Your father—"

"I already cleared it with him."

She studied his expression. "What's really going on?"

He hesitated before answering. "Nothing."

"I don't believe you."

"Nothing yet."

"You have another interview."

"The less said, the better. I refuse to put you in a position where you have to lie for me."

Dammit. He was being obstinate.

"Mommy!" Gretchen's call sounded closer and more urgent.

"Goodbye, Ryder."

Tatum left him standing there. As she hurried toward her children, she held her left hand out in front of her.

The cheap blue ring gathered the sun's rays and, for a split second, glinted brightly, more dazzling than any gold wedding band.

Sadly, the effect didn't linger. Like Ryder's affection for her, it was only fleeting.

RYDER NEEDED TO return to Phoenix to wrap up some loose ends. That, at least, was the excuse he'd given his family. Tatum heard it from Sunny. Not him. Truthfully, he'd kept scarce since the Wild West Days Rodeo.

It was for the best, she insisted. Their pretend wedding

may have been a farce, but her emotional reaction to it was real and, frankly, alarming.

A busy schedule had made avoiding Ryder, and protecting her heart, easy. The only time they'd talked was when he mentioned the meeting in Globe tomorrow with the potential new client. He was determined she accompany him and—what had he called it?—shadow him. She'd refused and assumed the subject was closed. Then, this morning, he'd sent her an email.

Groaning in frustration, Tatum pushed thoughts of Ryder from her mind. She had a lot of work piled on her desk, typical after a big rodeo. Final attendance numbers needed to be run. Contract laborers paid. Remaining funds deposited in the bank. Follow-up phone calls placed and photos uploaded to the website.

She welcomed the distraction. The school board was convening tomorrow and deciding on the new budget. Sunny had promised to inform Tatum of the voting outcome right away. She kept reminding herself it wasn't the end of the world if the school didn't rehire her. Her job at the arena wasn't unpleasant. More importantly, it enabled her to put a decent roof over her children's heads, albeit a small one.

So what if they didn't have a backyard to play in or the latest electronic learning devices? The wolf wasn't howling at their door anymore. And there were her art classes.

For the time being, that was. Until Lenny leased out her space. Perhaps she could find a new one…

Longing to teach full-time returned, an ever-growing void deep inside her. Managing an office, even a busy one, didn't give her the same satisfaction as standing in front of a classroom filled with bright, eager students ready to learn.

Maybe someday she'd teach again. *Yes*, someday, she promised herself. In Reckless or elsewhere. No reason she had to remain. Especially if Ryder left.

Hold on a minute! What did she care if he stayed or went? It had no bearing on her plans.

She cared because Ryder was important to the Becketts, and *they* mattered to her.

Returning to her computer, Tatum opened the spreadsheet she'd started earlier that day and began making entries. Mercer wanted to see how the various bucking stock performed based on the competitors' scores. Together, they'd designed a report that would give him the information in a concise, easy-to-read format. It was a task right up Sunny's alley, but Tatum was the one Mercer had asked for assistance.

Sunny said she was fine with it. Tatum thought otherwise.

As much as she loved the Becketts, she'd grown weary of their ceaseless squabbling. They sure knew how to make things hard on each other. Cassidy had told Tatum about Mercer's desire to purchase additional bulls. Sunny, of course, objected, and, as usual, the three siblings were taking sides and forming alliances. Though they were attempting to be civilized, tensions simmered just beneath the surface, and they were no fun to be around.

Then again, who was Tatum to talk? The Mayweathers were no better. She and Ruth hadn't spoken since Saturday. Monty, however, had called last night after two weeks of "radio silence." He'd asked about Drew's dislocated pinky, then pumped her for information on her personal life. Awkward!

Ruth must have put him up to it, and Monty went along. That he should take an interest only because another man was in the picture irked Tatum to no end. Weren't their children important enough on their own?

She winced as a headache chose that moment to make its presence known. Frankly, she didn't blame Ryder for his unexpected trip to Phoenix, if that was indeed where he'd gone. He could have flown out for the day to L.A. or even Denver to interview. She envied his ability leave all this stress behind.

She was just entering the last batch of numbers into the spreadsheet when the intercom rang. A quick check of the display confirmed her suspicions. Sunny was calling from the extension in the house. She often went there during lunch. Though, come to think of it, Tatum hadn't seen her boss all morning. Another Beckett mysteriously absent.

Picking up the receiver, she said, "Hi, Sunny."

"Hey, are you busy?"

"Not too bad. The phone's quieted down." It had been ringing off the hook most of the morning.

"Can you spare a few minutes?"

"Absolutely."

"Meet me in the house."

That was a strange request. "There's no one to cover the office."

"Put the phone on answering machine and lock the door."

Only someone who knew Sunny well would detect the strain in her voice. "Is something wrong?"

"Just come."

Her stomach in knots, Tatum did as requested. Her sense of doom increased as she crossed the backyard to the house.

"Hi," Tatum called, knocking as she entered the kitchen.

"We're in the living room."

We? Tatum passed through the connecting archway and had her answer. Lenny sat on the couch alongside Sunny. He stood at Tatum's approach.

"How you doing?" he asked, his tone kind.

Surprise rendered her speechless. Then, all at once, she knew. He was on the board with Sunny. This had something to do with her teaching job.

"Sit down." Sunny indicated an empty seat.

Moving in slow motion, Tatum managed to make it to the side chair and sit without falling to pieces.

"A conflict arose in the schedule," Sunny started. "The board decided to move up the budget meeting to today."

"You didn't tell me," Tatum murmured, annoyed at herself for missing the notices.

"We thought it best to wait."

Until the vote was taken, she silently finished for them. Because the majority of members didn't support allocating additional funds to hire more teachers.

"I'm sorry," Lenny said. "We fought as hard as we could."

"It's all right." Tatum swallowed. "I know you did."

"There'll be another budget meeting this spring." Sunny reached over and gave Tatum's hand a sympathetic squeeze.

Six months. It felt closer to a lifetime.

"A lot can happen between now and then," Lenny said.

"And, of course, you have your job here."

Her pity job, thanks to the Becketts' charity.

"Plus," Lenny added, "I'll talk to my landlord. See if he's willing to cut me a deal on the new lease."

They were being nice. And supportive. Not to acknowledge that would make Tatum appear unappreciative. Right now, at this juncture in her life, she needed the kindness of friends.

"Thank you." She stood, grabbing the chair arm for support. "You have both done so much for me."

"We love you, Tatum," Sunny said.

"If you'll excuse me, I'd like some time alone."

Sunny walked her to the kitchen door. "Take the rest of the day off if you want."

Tatum shook her head. "No. I'd rather work."

"I understand."

Sunny didn't. She probably figured Tatum wanted to keep busy so as not to dwell on the disappointing news. She was wrong.

Tatum's agenda for the afternoon had changed. Rather

than catch up on the post-rodeo paperwork, she was calling Ryder and telling him she'd be going with him to the meeting tomorrow in Globe.

Chapter Eleven

Being early made no difference. The restaurant Lynda Spencer had chosen for their lunch meeting was packed. After a five-minute wait spent sitting on a bench squeezed between a pair of elderly men and a trio of rowdy teenagers, they were led to a table.

"Is the entire population of Globe here today?" Tatum asked, half in jest, half serious.

"The food is supposed to be good."

She picked up the menu, intending to peruse it. Except, she was distracted. "Maybe not the best place for a meeting. It's pretty loud."

"Lynda raved about the barbeque pork."

Okay. Tatum was fast learning. If the client wanted to meet in a busy, crowded, noisy restaurant, then that was where they met.

Ryder checked his watch. "She won't be here until twelve-fifteen."

"Then why the rush?"

He'd insisted they hit the road, urging her to hurry when she wanted to finish updating the weekly calendar.

"I need to talk to you before Lynda gets here."

"About what?" Tatum's anxiety shot through the roof. She was already a wreck, fretting about the meeting all last evening and convincing herself the whole thing was a mistake. She was no sales person.

"I'd like you to take the lead today," Ryder said.

"What? No!"

"You conduct the meeting. I'll be your wing man."

She sat back, stunned. "I have zero experience. Repeat, zero."

"You've been helping me since I came home. With the secretary from the mining company and with Marshall Whitmen. Not to mention returning my messages, composing my correspondence and making cold calls to other rodeo arenas about reciprocal advertising."

"Not the same," she insisted.

"You'll do fine."

Tatum rubbed her damp palms along her skirt. "I can't possibly—"

"You can. You will."

"Why not tell me this on the drive over?" she snapped. Or yesterday, when she called him to say she'd changed her mind?

"Because I knew you'd be nervous."

"I am."

"And say no."

"Loud and clear, in case you haven't heard me yet."

"Tatum, listen to me." He waited for her to look at him, which she did reluctantly. "I went on an interview yesterday."

"I figured as much."

"The company is headquartered in Vegas with branches all over the country. Their HR team was in town recruiting, along with the VP of marketing."

She let that sink in. "Are you taking the job?"

"I might. If they offer it to me."

"Have you told your family yet?" She groaned. "You must think me a nag."

He ignored her question. "I heard about the school board vote. I'm sorry."

"Me, too. But what can I do except move on?" She shrugged. "Which is why I'm here with you today."

"I agree, and this meeting with Lynda is your chance to prove your worth to my parents. I have faith in you."

"I need more experience."

"I'll be right next to you the entire time. If you flounder, I'll step in. If you veer in the wrong direction, I'll steer you back on track. Just take your cues from me."

She shook her head vehemently.

"This is your chance, Tatum. Think about your kids. Wouldn't you like to be earning five thousand dollars a year more? That's what I'll tell my parents you're worth."

"Your dad won't pay it."

"We stand to make almost that much money on this contract alone if we land it. If *you* land it."

Tatum had her doubts. Mercer was beginning to warm up to her, it was true—they'd worked closely together this past week—but give her a five thousand dollar raise? Not happening.

"Once they see how well you do, they'll be on board."

Tatum drew in a deep breath. "I'm scared," she admitted.

"Of what? Failing or succeeding?"

"I want to be a teacher."

"Are you worried you'll find a career you like better than that?"

"That's not it. I'm afraid of…of…change."

He chuckled mirthlessly. "That Monty is a piece of work."

"What does he have to do with this?"

"He took all the fight out of you. The girl I remember was brave and strong and willing to go after what she wanted."

Like giving an older boy a homemade Valentine card?

"The divorce was hard." And what had happened since.

"Don't let it define you."

Her spine straightened. "I don't."

"Really?" Ryder's tone rang with challenge.

"I'll have you know I've bounced back from some pretty dire circumstances."

A slow grin spread across his face. "That's my girl. You'll be amazing."

She gawked at him. "You did that on purpose. Goaded me."

"Consider it a pep talk."

"I ought to…"

He silenced her with a subtle wave. "Save it for later. Here comes Lynda."

Tatum's resolve faltered. But only momentarily. Like yesterday right after Sunny delivered the news about the school board vote, it returned with a vengeance and filled her with determination.

She could do this. Better herself for her children's sakes. Tatum was good with people. And smart. Creative. And, like Ryder said, he'd be right there, stepping in if need be.

When Lynda Spencer reached their table, Tatum rose first to greet the smartly dressed woman and held out her hand. "Ms. Spencer. It's a real pleasure to meet you. I'm Tatum Mayweather with the Easy Money."

TATUM LEFT THE restaurant walking on air. Oh, she'd flubbed up during the meeting. More than once. Not terribly, though. And as promised, Ryder had jumped in to rescue her. She couldn't say she'd led the meeting, but she'd contributed. Greatly. The final contract terms had been her suggestion, further encouraged by Ryder's imperceptible nod of approval.

Lynda—she and Tatum were on a first-name basis now—hadn't even asked for a formal letter of intent. Rather, she'd told Tatum to forward the completed contract at her earliest convenience.

No wonder Ryder loved his job. She, too, could get used to this amazing elation at the close of every deal. It wasn't the same sense of satisfaction that teaching gave her. Far different, in fact. It was, however, rewarding and fulfilling. She'd missed the feeling.

"Nice grin," Ryder said as they wove through the parking lot toward his truck.

She had the humility to look chagrined. "Sorry."

"Don't be." He went around and opened the passenger door for her. "You have every right to gloat. Heck, I'd be gloating, too, if I were you."

"I can honestly say you taught me everything I know."

"I'm recommending my folks give you a bonus when Lynda returns the signed contract."

"That's not necessary."

"No guarantee. But they need to know how well you did."

She paused. The words she'd intended to utter died on her lips when she realized she was caught between Ryder and the truck's interior. Not trapped exactly but... contained, his strong arms bracketing her sides.

A sudden warmth pooled in her middle. She would have attributed it to the warm afternoon if not for the light-headedness that increased the closer he got.

Struggling to bring a calm to the abrupt storm of emotions, she said, "I'll run the draft contract by you before giving it to Mercer."

"I'm sure it'll be fine." He dipped his head. Only a fraction of an inch but enough to ignite a delicious thrill.

Was he going to kiss her? A small, silent voice inside her pleaded, *yes, yes.*

"I hope you don't mind," he said, his voice trailing off.

"What?" Take her to dinner? Take her home? Take her in his arms?

"I have a stop to make on the way out of town."

"A stop?" She leaned involuntarily toward him.

Ryder did the same and reached behind her. Only instead of pulling her against him, he removed the portfolio he'd left on the seat and dropped it to the floor.

"The hardware store. I told Dad I'd pick up some light-bulbs and salt pellets for the water softener. He's helping Mom with chores at the house."

So much for spontaneous romantic gestures. Ryder backed away, and, when she climbed onto the truck seat, he closed the door behind her.

Good grief. She was such an idiot, reading meaning into a meaningless comment. What had she been thinking? That he wanted to stop for flowers and a bottle of wine? Hardly.

With all the casualness she could muster, Tatum continued the conversation, as if Sunny's honey-do list was absolutely riveting. "Chores for your mom?"

"Yeah. Dad's trying to get in her good graces." Ryder sent her a wry look. "He's hell-bent on remarrying her."

"Cassidy told me." She'd talked Tatum's ear off one night well into the wee hours. Tatum had listened and given what counsel she could.

"She's not happy about it," Ryder observed, "but Liberty's overjoyed."

"What about you?"

"My parents' love life is none of my business."

The three Beckett siblings divided, as always. Was he, like Cassidy, not in favor of a reconciliation? Tatum could see both sides. Sunny and Mercer were a great team, even if they did disagree from time to time. Plus, they had a long history together, not all of it unhappy.

On the flip side, Sunny had lied to her entire family about Mercer being Liberty's father. It was a lot to sweep under the carpet. A lot to forgive.

Ryder turned the truck into a small plaza. She had been there more times than she could count. A couple doors down from the hardware store was a hobby shop with its gaily painted windows advertising specials. Before the school had laid her off, she'd made a monthly trek to the hobby shop in search of classroom and art supplies.

"Come on." Ryder beckoned when Tatum hesitated. "It's too hot to sit in the truck."

He was right.

Groaning to herself, she flung open the passenger door and got out. Did she have to continually turn a good time into a bad time simply because she'd misinterpreted something Ryder said?

"Tatum. Hi."

At the familiar voice behind her, she spun. "Maggie. Hello." She stopped to speak to her friend. "Don't you have class this afternoon?"

"There's an assembly next week, and I volunteered to make a supply run." Maggie carried a large sack with the hobby shop's trademark logo in each hand.

"Looks like you bought out the entire store."

"I figured I'd make the gas count." She eyed Ryder with curiosity. "Hello, have we met before?"

"Ryder Beckett." He smiled.

"Of course. I should have guessed. You look like your father." Her smile widened to include Tatum. "Are all the Beckett men heartbreakers?"

Tatum forced herself not to react. Inside, she worried that her attraction to Ryder was obvious to anyone who bothered to look closely.

The three of them visited for several minutes. Before leaving, Maggie told Tatum, "We miss you at the school."

"I miss everyone there, too."

"I'd best get going." She switched both bags to one hand in order to give Tatum a hug. "It's a long drive home, and I have supper to get on the table."

In the hardware store Tatum followed Ryder from aisle to aisle, still feeling a little uncomfortable and put out. At the truck, he loaded his purchases into the bed, the heavy bag of salt pellets landing with a thud.

"If you opened your store," he said, "your friends wouldn't have to drive into Globe."

"There's no chance of that happening."

"Not with you doing as great as you did today."

She'd been thinking more about a lack of finances.

They didn't talk much after that, and Tatum let her gaze aimlessly travel the streets of town. Ryder's sharp right turn startled her out of her reverie.

"Where are we going?"

"The marina," he answered without preamble.

"To take down our rodeo poster from their window?"

"They don't need us for that."

"Then, what?"

He clammed up. Tatum was just beginning to get annoyed when he entered the marina lot. Instead of parking near the quaint, nautical-style building with its life preservers hanging from the roof eaves, he drove to the north edge and the lakeshore.

"Ryder."

"I thought we'd play hooky for a bit." He opened his door and stepped out. "Come on, Tatum. Walk with me. It's beautiful out."

It was. Bright afternoon sun reflected off the rippling water, splintering into a million flickering diamonds.

When she hesitated, he said, "I want to explain. About what happened at my old job and why I really need to find another one."

That, she decided, was worth playing hooky for.

Chapter Twelve

Revealing the biggest blunder of one's life wasn't easy. Revealing it to a woman you cared about took it to the next level.

In the parking lot of the hardware store, Ryder had nearly kissed Tatum. Would have kissed her if given the chance. Fortunately, he'd stopped himself in the nick of time, before heaping mistake upon mistake.

His mother was right; Tatum had been through a lot and was practically raising her three children alone. She needed her job at the arena. More so now that the board had voted against rehiring her. He couldn't mess things up for her by getting personally involved. There was too much at stake.

Beneath their feet, the pontoon dock swayed and creaked like the moving floor of a carnival fun house. When it appeared Tatum might lose her balance, Ryder grabbed her elbow and steadied her.

"These aren't the best shoes for a dock."

He glanced down at the delicate black sandals, her painted toenails peeking out from beneath the straps. Feminine and very sexy and about as far removed from cowboy boots as possible. He wondered what her feet would look like bare and nestled next to his.

"I like your shoes," he said.

A bench was anchored to the end of the dock, large enough for two adults if they sat elbow to elbow.

Ryder gestured, and Tatum gratefully wobbled over to it.

She pulled the folds of her frilly skirt tight to her legs before sitting. It was also feminine and very sexy.

Ryder gave a low moan. Tatum could break down every one of his defenses just with the clothes she wore.

He sat beside her. The bench rocked sharply before settling. In the distance, a speed boat zoomed past. At the marina store, a group of fishermen ambled inside, poles and tackle boxes clasped in their hands. Water birds flew overhead, clustered together in a small flock. The next instant, they changed direction and drifted to the lake's surface in a graceful, seemingly choreographed, dance. Touching down, they dunked their heads completely under water in search of a meal.

"It's beautiful." Tatum's eyes widened as she took in the sights. "I can't remember my last trip to the lake. It's not far. I should bring the kids here more often."

She was rambling, his suggestion that they talk obviously unnerving her. Well, she had nothing on him. Ryder's mouth was bone dry, and the air felt too thin to breathe.

"I didn't quit Madison-Monroe," he finally said. "Okay, I did quit, but only because if I refused, I'd have been fired."

"Fired?" She studied him with interest, not judgment.

"And slapped with a lawsuit."

"What happened?"

"I was accused of inappropriate conduct." He swallowed again. "By one of my female team members."

"I don't believe it."

He'd been expecting her to recoil. Find him repulsive. Certainly be shocked. Instead, she'd defended him. That wouldn't last when she heard the details.

"Within the span of a week, I went from being head marketing exec of a large ad agency to being out of a job and pretty much unemployable."

"That's a serious charge. Why would she accuse you?" Trust Tatum to bypass the superficial and get to the crux of the matter.

"I did touch her. On the arm. It could have been construed as inappropriate."

"Was it inappropriate?"

"We dated. When I ended things, she became angry."

Tatum listened quietly as Ryder explained the details of his office romance, the messy breakup and messier aftermath. He tried to be as honest as possible and not paint himself as the victim, though that was how he felt.

"I screwed up," he concluded.

"You did."

Apparently, she was through defending him.

"You shouldn't have touched her arm. Not at the office and not in front of other people. Other than that…" She exhaled slowly. "There's always risk in crossing professional boundaries. The school has a strict no-fraternizing policy. I suppose with good reason."

"Which is why I wanted to talk to you," he said.

"About the school's policies?"

"About us. This attraction we have." He waited until her gaze met his. It was guarded. "We work together. Seeing each other, engaging in any relationship other than platonic, is not a good idea."

She pondered for several moments before answering. "The arena is different from most work places. It's impossible to separate personal relationships from professional ones. The owners are former husband and wife. Their three children work for them. Cassidy and I are best friends. Your mom is like a second mother to me. Liberty is marrying a former employee, who also happens to be the arena's legal counsel. I don't think it's possible to cross more professional boundaries than those."

"Are you saying you think it's all right for us to date?"

"No, I'm not. But for different reasons."

He took a stab in the not so dark. "Because I'm leaving."

A flash of anguish shone in her eyes. "I've already been abandoned by one man."

"I wouldn't hurt you, Tatum. Not intentionally and not if I could help it."

"I believe you." She offered up a tentative smile. "And I appreciate you telling me what really happened at Madison-Monroe."

"I thought you should know."

It did explain a lot.

Tatum glanced over her shoulder at the parking lot. "We should probably get going."

"That's right. You have to pick up the kids."

"Actually, it's Cassidy's turn. She's dropping Gretchen off at the boys' day care for me. One of the other children is having a birthday, and they're throwing a small party. I'm free until seven-thirty."

"What are you going to do with all that extra time?"

"I'm not sure. Maybe sit down and have an uninterrupted dinner for once. Read a book." She sounded almost gleeful. "Watch a grown-up TV show."

Ryder was both glad and relieved that they were back on an even keel. Perhaps they could remain friends after all.

At the arena, they each returned to work. Tatum hit the office, and Ryder reported the good news about Lynda Spencer and the new contract to his father.

"Tatum did well today," he said.

"Taking notes again?"

"Actually, she led the meeting." Tatum might disagree, but Ryder believed differently.

"You put her in charge?" Frown lines creased his father's brow. "This could be an important new client."

"Tatum negotiated the terms. Lynda agreed to them. She's expecting a contract ASAP and committed to signing it. Tatum's drawing up the paperwork now."

"You're coaching her?"

"*Mentoring* her is a better word."

"Why bother?"

His father set the rake aside. He'd been cleaning horse

stalls in the main barn. It was a task normally performed by one of the hands, typically the lowest on the totem pole. But Mercer Beckett wasn't above helping out in any capacity when needed, and, at the moment, they were shorthanded.

"She has potential. And I won't be available for long. She could fill in for me."

"You find a new job yet?"

Here was a perfect opening if Ryder ever saw one. "I've been approached by a couple of companies looking for an account exec."

"Is this because of the argument we had last week?"

"I'm glad to be home, Dad. I appreciate everything you've done for me. But let's be honest. You've created a position where there wasn't one. A position that, between you and Tatum, isn't entirely necessary."

"We're growing. Every week. I may have created the position, but it won't be long before we can't run this place without you."

"You're cleaning stalls, Dad. Hire another wrangler and you're going to have plenty of time to do my job."

"I called Harlo Billings this morning and put in an offer on those bulls and heifers."

"Mom agreed?"

"She didn't disagree."

It occurred to Ryder that his father may have another agenda. "I don't want your half of the arena."

"What are you talking about?"

"Cassidy and Liberty will take over the Easy Money when you and Mom retire. Not me. You can't dangle part ownership like a carrot on a string and expect me to bite."

"That's a crock of horse crap if I ever heard one."

"It isn't, and you know it." Ryder tried a different approach, one that would strike a chord with his father. "You're paying me a good wage. Think how much livestock you could buy instead."

"We could increase to five rodeos a year. Generate more revenue."

"Come on. Be reasonable."

His father grunted.

"I took this job only until I got my feet under me," Ryder said. "And to make you happy."

"I don't want you to leave."

That was closer to the truth. "Whatever happens, Dad, I won't stay away like before. I'm committed to reuniting this family and returning often. Besides, I haven't said yes to anyone yet."

Ryder's father pulled him into a fierce and unexpected hug. "I reckon you have to do what's best for you. Much as I'd like the Easy Money to be your calling, it obviously isn't."

"I love this place. I always have. But I want to, need to, work for a company where I can make a real difference. Where my contributions are valued. Where I *earn* my keep."

"You can do that here, son."

Ryder wasn't convinced. "You're the driving force behind the changes and growth. I'm just riding your coattails."

"I don't see it that way."

But Ryder did, and, in the end, that was what counted.

Later that afternoon, he returned to the office to find it empty. His mother was helping Liberty set up for the team penning practice starting at five. Tatum had already left for the day.

Using the computer at her desk, Ryder checked his emails, answering the urgent ones and leaving the remainder until tomorrow. Next, he returned a half dozen phone calls. During the last one, his cell phone rang. It was Myra.

"Good news," she announced in a chipper voice. "The head of HR from Velocity Concepts called. They've made you an offer."

The company Ryder had interviewed with yesterday. "That was fast."

"Apparently you were heads and tails above the other candidates."

Unlike the interview last week, this job was a good fit. Velocity Concepts had been formed fewer than three years ago. The founders were young, aggressive and innovative. He'd get in mostly on the ground floor.

"Which branch office?" The recruiter had mentioned several.

"Here's the best part," Myra said. "They want you for the northwest Phoenix location."

Not next door to Reckless but less than a two-hour drive, depending on traffic. Very doable, Ryder decided.

For what? Keeping his promise to his father that he wouldn't stay away like before? Getting to know Liberty and Benjie better. Dating Tatum?

Why not? He and Tatum would no longer be coworkers, and she could feel assured he wasn't going away. Excitement coursed through him.

Myra's mention of the offered salary jolted Ryder from his mental wanderings. He asked her to repeat the amount.

"That's not as much as I'd hoped."

"We can always ask for more. But, considering your circumstances and the current job market, it's doubtful you'll be able to get as much as you were earning at Madison-Monroe."

Ryder read between the lines. His "little mistake" had cost him dearly and was forcing him to start lower on the pay-scale ladder. Being prepared for such an outcome didn't lessen the sting.

"Look at the pluses." Myra continued selling the company by listing the many positive aspects.

"Email me the offer," he said. "I'll look at it tonight." And likely accept it, he told himself.

"I'm sending it as we speak."

"Thanks, Myra, for believing in me." He'd needed someone in his corner, and she'd been there.

"They want an answer within forty-eight hours."

Ryder was already heading toward the office door. "I'll
call you by nine tomorrow."

He'd long left the arena and was driving in the direction of town before admitting to himself his destination.

Tatum's apartment was easy to find. He'd looked up
her address a few days ago. At his loud knock, she called,
"Coming," and a moment later, opened the door.

His jaw literally dropped. She'd changed from her work
clothes into teeny shorts and a snug T-shirt that outlined
every curve of her hourglass figure.

"Is something wrong?" she asked.

"Something's right." He scanned her face, wanting to
see her reaction.

"What?"

"Invite me in, Tatum. I have news."

OUT OF HABIT, Tatum searched the small living room for her
children. Then, she remembered. They were at the birthday party and would be for—she checked the wall clock—
two more hours.

"What news?" She shifted uncomfortably. There was no
reason for her to feel incredibly nervous and vulnerable.

Yet, she did. For she was truly alone with Ryder. For the
first time since they were young. Possibly ever.

She trusted him. Of course she did. His kisses hadn't
been inappropriate. It was herself she didn't trust. Not when
his sexy smile melted her resolve and caused her heart rate
to quicken.

"The company I told you about, they came back with a
formal offer," he said. "A decent one."

She went over to the couch and sat, trying not to think
of what this meant for her and what a good opportunity

it could be for him. A chance to rebuild his career, which was important to him.

Still, shock rippled through her like a small quake. He'd be leaving any day. She was bereft already.

"Where?" she asked, amazed at her composure.

"Velocity Concepts."

Removing his cowboy hat and setting it on the coffee table, he joined her on the couch—which usually felt plenty big, even with her entire brood piled upon it. Ryder, however, took up most of the available space. Not crowding her but making her acutely aware of his presence. Her body responded despite her mind's strict instruction to remain indifferent.

"I'm not familiar with them." Frankly, she wasn't familiar with any marketing company.

"They're relatively new but with an impressive portfolio of clients."

She'd wanted to know where the company was located, not their name. Perhaps it was best that he'd misunderstood her. Then he wouldn't see the depths of her disappointment at his leaving.

"Well, good luck." What else was there to say?

"This is a positive thing, Tatum."

Was it? Probably. She'd secretly pined after Ryder since his return. But despite their passionate kisses, she doubted he really wanted her. Not in the way she craved to be wanted. Desire differed from love or even genuine affection. Desire didn't demand a commitment.

Perhaps the story about his coworker was simply an excuse, one he'd given to let her down easy rather than admit he wasn't emotionally available.

"How did your family react?"

"I haven't told them yet. I came here first. I figure I'll break it to them at our staff meeting on Friday morning. After I've formally accepted the offer. I did tell Dad I was looking for a job."

She would beg off the meeting, she decided. Better than having to sit through the news a second time. Sunny, she was sure, would be watching her for any response.

"Your mom and sisters will be upset." At his leaving, of course. But Sunny had also been hoping for, counting on, a reconciliation.

"I promised Dad I'd come back often. It won't be like before."

"I'm glad for you," she said with all the sincerity she could muster. She'd seen this coming. Ryder had warned her repeatedly. Nonetheless, it hurt.

"You could be glad for *us*."

"Us?"

He slid closer, the cushions dipping beneath his weight. If she wasn't mistaken, his eyes darkened as they fastened on her. The vulnerability she'd felt earlier gave way to awareness.

"We won't be coworkers anymore," he said, his gaze intense. "We can see each other without crossing any of those boundaries you mentioned."

"See each other?" She felt like a parrot, repeating everything he said.

"Date. I want to go out with you, Tatum."

She turned away, fearing her expression reflected too much of her feelings. How was it Ryder could disarm her simply with a look?

"You'll be far away. I can't handle a long-distance relationship."

"Phoenix isn't that far."

She stared at him in amazement. "The job's local?"

"Local enough. Off the 101 and the 17."

Tatum was familiar with the area, having driven past it dozens of times on her way to her ex-mother-in-law's house in Glendale.

"I won't leave you, Tatum," he stated. "Not like Monty did."

For a moment, she dreamed. Until reality returned. "You can't make that kind of promise. Truthfully, we don't know each other well. You've only been home a few weeks."

He rested an arm on the back of the couch, his fingers finding and sifting through the long strands of her hair. "That's the purpose of dating. To get better acquainted."

She should ask for time to think about it. "How soon? Until you take the job at Velocity?"

"I'm requesting two weeks. That should give me enough time to teach you more about my job and to convince Mom and Dad that you deserve a raise. You'll get that bigger place to live, Tatum."

A sudden thought unraveled her. "You're not doing this for me, are you? Taking the job? Because I won't—"

"I'm not. But neither am I ignoring the benefits. For both of us."

Wasn't this what she'd always hoped for? A chance to be with Ryder *and* the ability to earn more income? What in the world was holding her back? She should be throwing herself at him.

"I'm high maintenance. You'll probably regret getting involved with me."

He laughed. "Not possible."

"Seriously. I have three children. You haven't begun to see them at their worst. And a nosy, interfering ex-mother-in-law."

"I happen to like your kids. And your mother-in-law doesn't scare me."

"But are you ready for a family? I don't think so," she answered before he could. "And I don't date casually."

"Okay."

"Really? Because there's no other way I'll consider going out with you. Not saying I need a gold ring, but I do need a serious commitment."

If she'd thought to dissuade him, she thought wrong.

Reaching over, he pulled her into an embrace. "I want that, too, sweetheart."

She was desperate to believe him. Nothing would make her happier.

"Two weeks." He leaned in and brushed his lips across her cheek. "Let's date until I leave for my new job. It'll be like a test run."

She resisted. "You're not a car I'm thinking about buying."

His lips moved to her mouth. "Take a chance, Tatum," Ryder said against her lips before covering them in a crushing kiss.

The compelling evidence of his desire pressed into her leg as he eased her backward onto the couch cushions, his mouth tasting the sensitive skin of her neck. Softly uttered endearments filled her ears.

Gorgeous. Sexy. Incredible. She hadn't felt any of those things in a long, long time.

Wait. That wasn't true. She'd felt them and more each time Ryder had kissed her. He'd told her with his lips and words and touch that she was much more than an overworked, dowdy mother and office employee. With him, she was a sultry and sensuous beauty.

"Have dinner with me on Friday." His breath was warm, and his masculine scent filled her senses.

"The kids." She opened her eyes, momentarily disorientated.

"Ask Cassidy to watch them."

"All right." How could she say no? Impossible with him tugging her earlobe into his mouth.

Another deep, incredible kiss left her limbs boneless. Oh, dear. What would making love with him be like? Tatum had an overwhelming urge to find out.

"I'll pick you up at seven," he said. "There's a new band playing at the Hole in the Wall."

"You dance?" She hadn't been in years.

"I won't embarrass you."

"You could never do that." She thought of being in his arms, gliding across the dance floor to the strains of a slow song. Suddenly, she couldn't wait.

"Unless you want to go into Globe instead. Then, let's make it six-thirty."

"I don't care." She didn't. "The Hole in the Wall is fine."

All she wanted was to be with Ryder. Experience the heaven he could take her to in three seconds flat. To that end, she arched against him, expecting another kiss and perhaps a hand exploring the parts of her body left too long unattended. Instead, he pushed away from her and practically jumped to his feet.

"Ryder?" She blinked, stupidly she was sure. "What's wrong?"

"I should go." Something akin to desperation filled his eyes. Or, was it frustration?

She took the hand he offered and rose. "So soon? The kids won't be home for a while."

Heat seemed to radiate off him. "If I stay, I'm going to want to do more than kiss you, Tatum."

His words poured over her and ignited a thrill. "What if I want you to stay?"

The heat intensified. "Think about what you're saying."

"I am."

"I won't ruin what we have by moving too fast."

He made perfect sense. Tatum didn't want to ruin what they had, either. But neither did she want him to go.

"I've been simply existing for years now. Making it through every day as best I can." She looped her arms around his shoulders and lifted her face to his. "You make me feel special, Ryder. You've opened doors for me. Shown me that there's a life out there waiting to be lived."

He lowered his head until their lips were a hairsbreadth apart. "You need to be absolutely sure. I won't take you to bed any other way."

"Who knows what tomorrow will bring? This could be the start of an amazing future or just the best two weeks of my life. Regardless, I'm going to enjoy the time we have without regrets."

When Ryder moved to kiss her again, she retreated. His look of question turned to raw hunger when she clasped his hand and led him down the hall to her bedroom.

Chapter Thirteen

Ryder's hands on her naked body. Strong. Firm. Possessive. Eliciting seductive moans and tiny shudders from her, then an exhilarating climax. Without being told, he'd understood where to touch her, how much pressure to apply and that kisses and nibbles along the base of her neck drove her absolutely crazy.

Tatum had imagined this, being with Ryder. She was human, after all, and a woman. But even her best fantasies hadn't come close to the real thing.

Before undressing her, he'd produced a condom. She didn't ask why he carried one in his wallet. She was just glad he'd brought one. After pleasuring her expertly and thoroughly with his mouth and hands, he'd placed the condom over his impressive erection.

She'd done that to him, she thought with no small degree of satisfaction. Brought him to a fully aroused state with nothing more than her utter abandon.

Ryder, she'd learned, liked watching the results of his efforts. His eyes had remained riveted on her face in the semidarkness as he'd coaxed one exquisite response after the other from her. Tatum discovered that she, too, liked watching. Seeing his eyes fill with desire. His jaw muscles tense and flex from the strain of holding back. His chest rise and fall in rhythm to her own rapid breathing.

She intended to return the favor when he finished with the condom. He no sooner collapsed onto the pillows than she slung a leg over his hips and straddled him.

"Baby," was all he got out before she wrapped her fingers around him and guided him inside her. After that, he communicated only in groans and deep exhalations.

"Tell me," she demanded. "How does it feel?"

His response was to grab hold of her waist and bury himself inside her.

"Tell me," she repeated.

"Like nothing else. Smooth. Slick. Intense." He punctuated the last word with a desperate sound from someplace low in his throat.

Tatum smiled. She wanted this experience to be like nothing else. Whatever happened between them, and she vowed to be a realist, this night, this moment would be one of a kind. For both of them.

Leaning forward, she brought her breasts to his mouth. He suckled each one, the pressure he applied building as did the power of his thrusts. When she could take no more, she pulled away, denying him. He swore under his breath, then released an anguished hiss when she reached between their bodies and let her fingers play. Ryder lasted only a few seconds longer before his release crashed down on the both of them with startling force. Even before the last tremor subsided, he pulled her down to meet his mouth in a searing kiss that went on and on and on.

"You're amazing." He cradled her face in his hands.

"You're not so bad yourself."

"I was worried."

"About what?"

"Pleasing you."

No one had ever pleased her more. "Couldn't you tell?"

"I thought so. I admit to getting a bit lost for a while there."

Love talk. Tatum started to think she'd missed it, then wondered if she'd ever really engaged in it before. No, not like this.

Several seconds passed before either of them moved or

spoke again. Eventually, Tatum eased herself off Ryder and stretched out next to him, their legs entwined and her head resting on his shoulder. Perfect and peaceful. Too bad it couldn't last.

"I hate to break up the party." She trailed her fingers through his thick chest hair and down his belly, enjoying his sharp intake of breath. "But the kids will be home soon."

"I'll leave."

She propped herself up on one elbow to stare at him. "Get dressed, at least. I can come up with a reason for you being here. Not for us frolicking with our pants down."

He didn't immediately spring from bed. "I need you to know something, Tatum."

"All right." The seriousness of his tone worried her.

"Whatever you may think of my past, I don't take sex lightly." He tucked a lock of her hair behind her ear. "You're important to me. Very. More than you can imagine."

"Good." She let herself relax. "Because you're important to me, too."

"I won't say anything to anyone about tonight. You can trust me."

"I'm not ashamed."

"Neither am I, but I don't want people getting the wrong impression."

His argument had merit. "I think we should tell your parents we're dating. We both work for them, after all. For the time being."

He swung his legs onto the floor and stood. She couldn't resist and took a moment to admire his toned, athletic build. Ryder may work as a marketing executive, but he had the hard, sculpted body of a man who earned his living outdoors.

"I'll leave that to you," he said solemnly.

"Are you uncomfortable with telling them?"

He yanked her to her feet and into his arms. "I couldn't be prouder. Or happier."

"Maybe we can tell them together."

"I'd like that." He smiled, and her heart dissolved into a puddle of mush.

It was a fact of life. While undressing and making love had been natural and easy, dressing was somehow a little awkward. Particularly when she turned on the light in order for them to locate their clothes.

Tatum slipped on her shorts from earlier. Certain her face shone beet-red, she averted her gaze. A moment later, Ryder came up behind her. Wrapping his arms around her waist, he rested his chin on the top of her head.

"Can I call you later?" he asked.

"Tonight?"

"Yes, tonight." He nuzzled her ear. "And tomorrow when you wake up."

Hearing Ryder's voice first thing in the morning? Just like that, the awkwardness perhaps only she'd been feeling evaporated.

"Okay." More than okay. It was wonderful.

She walked him to the door. Ignoring the neighbor who'd come out to dispose of her trash in the communal Dumpster, Ryder kissed Tatum. It was less intimate, less sensuous than when they'd been making love, yet a languid sigh escaped her. If only it could be like this always.

"See you tomorrow, sweetheart."

Sweetheart. She liked the rich timbre of his voice when he spoke the endearment.

Ryder wasn't gone five minutes when Cassidy showed up with all four children. Tatum went from quietly indulging herself in memories to fending off a friendly assault of hugs and kisses, accompanied by cries of "Mommy, can I watch TV?" and "Drew hit me in the arm with his cast."

A pile of inexpensive trinkets, bounty from the birthday party, appeared in the middle of the living room floor.

"How were they?" she asked Cassidy.

Her friend stopped dead in her tracks and gave Tatum a long and thorough once-over. "What happened to you?"

"Nothing?"

"You are so lying."

"I swear. I'm fine."

"I can see that. You're glowing."

Was she? Tatum grinned.

"Tell me," Cassidy insisted.

"Kids, clean up this mess. Then, get ready for a shower."

The three older children emitted cries of disappointment as they reluctantly gathered up the strewn trinkets. Adam crawled on to the couch and flopped over in the exact spot Ryder had been sitting when he first kissed Tatum. Right before she'd asked him to stay.

"How come Benjie doesn't have to take a shower?" Drew complained.

"I'm sure he does. At home."

Cassidy completely ignored Tatum's subtle hint that it was time to go. "Was Ryder here?"

"What makes you say that?" Tatum answered, a bit too quickly and too defensively.

"He wasn't at the arena. Dad says he's been AWOL for a while now and won't answer his phone."

"Maybe he had an appointment."

Good thing the older kids had disappeared into the bedrooms and Adam was half-asleep, because Cassidy refused to cease her interrogation.

"I thought I was your friend. Your *best* friend."

"You are."

"Then come clean. It's obvious you're happy. If that glow is Ryder's responsibility…well, he's my brother. I think I have a right to know."

Tatum looked around again, making sure no one seven years of age and under was listening. "He was here."

"And?"

"We're going out. This weekend. To the Hole in the Wall."

Cassidy nodded mutely.

"Does that bother you?"

"No. Yes."

"What's wrong, Cassidy?"

"He's not a relationship kind of guy."

"Maybe he's changed. He was married once."

"And done nothing but dated casually since. Every phone call I'd ask, and he'd answer the same. There was no one special. I'd hate to see you hurt."

"Rest assured, I'm going into this with my eyes wide open." Of course, Tatum was hoping, not so secretly, that Ryder was becoming more and more a relationship kind of guy. "It's just a date. Let's not get carried away."

"What date?"

Both Tatum and Cassidy whirled to see Gretchen standing not ten feet away.

"I'll explain later, sweet pea."

"Tell me now."

"Don't you have spelling words to study?" When her daughter refused to budge, Tatum said, "We'll talk after Cassidy and Benjie leave."

"Is Mr. Beckett your new boyfriend?"

Tatum made a practice of being painfully honest with her children when possible, something their father wasn't. Now, however, she chose to massage the truth.

"He and I are just going out. It's too soon to call him my boyfriend."

Anger distorted Gretchen's features as she cried out and bolted straight to her bedroom. The next thing Tatum heard was the door slamming.

"Oh, dear," Cassidy said.

All the joy Tatum felt the past hour left her in a rush. "I should go to her."

"I'll get out of your hair." She cupped her hands around her mouth and hollered, "Benjie. Let's get a move on."

Benjie dragged his feet. Eventually, mother and son were headed toward the door.

Cassidy hugged Tatum. "Call me if you need anything."

"She'll be okay."

"Mom dating is a big adjustment."

Cassidy spoke as if she knew, which was funny, considering she never dated.

"You okay?" Tatum opened Gretchen's bedroom door and stuck her head inside.

Her daughter lay on her twin bed, a stuffed bear clutched in her arms. As Tatum advanced into the room, Gretchen rolled over and faced the wall.

Sitting on the edge of the bed, Tatum said, "Please, don't be mad at me. I was going to tell you." She rubbed Gretchen's back, a leftover gesture from when her daughter was a tiny baby.

"Do you like him?" Gretchen's voice sounded small and uncertain.

"Yes, I do. And he likes you. Drew and Adam, too. I'm hoping you'll give him a chance. He's a very nice man."

Gretchen squeezed the stuffed bear tighter. "Is he going to be my new daddy?"

"Absolutely not. No one will ever replace Daddy."

"Lisa Anne's mommy has a new boyfriend."

Her playmate from school. Tatum heard the name often.

"And then her daddy went away."

"That won't happen."

"It might. If Mr. Beckett becomes your boyfriend."

"Your daddy loves you." Even as Tatum said the words, she doubted them. Monty was the slowly disappearing parent, and it had nothing to do with Ryder.

"I hate him."

"Don't say that! Daddy may not see you often—"

"Not him. I hate Mr. Beckett."

At her daughter's pitiful outcry, Tatum's heart broke. Gretchen's anger and resentment at Ryder had nothing to do with him and everything to do with her poor excuse for a father. She was simply too young to understand the difference. Unfortunately, Tatum's relationship with Ryder could—and probably would—suffer because of it. She didn't want that to happen, but family came first.

"We'll call Daddy tonight, okay? Find out when he's coming to Phoenix next and where he's staying, then drive over to see him."

"Promise?" Gretchen's eyes glistened with unshed tears.

"Absolutely."

Tatum refused to think about what would happen if Monty came up with his usual bunch of excuses.

"What's wrong?"

At Ryder's sudden appearance, Tatum involuntarily jerked and banged her knee on the open cabinet drawer. She hadn't heard him come into the office. That was what she got for letting her thoughts consume her.

"Why do you think something's wrong?"

"You've been hiding all day."

"I have not." She closed the cabinet drawer and faced him. "We talked this morning. Twice."

Ryder had called her shortly after her alarm went off and again on her way to the arena after she'd dropped the kids at school and day care. His timing had been good, which showed he paid attention to the small details of her life. It was flattering and sweet. And the kind of thing a boyfriend would do.

She'd cut him short. Both times.

Gretchen's tearful outburst resounded in Tatum's head. Her poor little daughter had gone to bed unhappy when their call to Monty went unanswered and the voice-mail message they'd left unreturned.

"I looked for you at lunch," Ryder said.

"I had some errands to run."

"You left? I didn't notice."

"Cassidy and I drove together."

He studied her critically. "What's really bothering you?"

"I'm just busy." She started for her desk. Luckily, the office was empty and no one was listening. Unluckily, Tatum couldn't use unwanted eyes and ears as an excuse to have this conversation later.

"Tatum, sweetheart. Tell me. What chance do we have if you won't communicate?"

The tender look in his eyes was her undoing.

"Gretchen's worried that, because of you, Monty will stop coming around. She doesn't want to lose her father."

"Monty stopped coming around long before I entered the picture."

"She's young. She has trouble comprehending a complicated situation."

"What can I do to make it better?" He lifted his hand to her cheek.

Tatum closed her eyes and abandoned herself to the sensation his caress evoked. "Be patient."

"We are still going out this weekend."

Her eyes snapped open. "About that…"

"Don't say you've reconsidered."

"I have to think of my children."

"The boys like me. We're pals."

"Gretchen's sensitive. She's the oldest and misses Monty the most."

"I get it. It was the same for me when my dad left."

Not entirely. His mother had insisted his father leave. And it was a well-known fact Mercer would have visited his children much more frequently if Sunny had allowed it. Monty, on the other hand, had been the one to do the leaving. And he'd rather be anywhere else besides Reckless.

"I won't take no for an answer," Ryder said. "I'm picking you up at seven on Friday."

Her defenses rose. She didn't like being put in a difficult position. "Please, don't make me choose."

"Don't use Gretchen as an excuse."

She drew back, astounded. "I beg your pardon."

"If you're having doubts about us, Tatum, say so. Don't make Gretchen the scapegoat."

"I'm not." She pressed a hand to her forehead. "Okay, maybe I am having a few doubts."

"That's better." A small smile lifted the corners of his mouth.

"How is that better?"

"We can deal with doubts. Overcome them. As long as you're honest."

"This is new for me. Dating post-divorce and with children who are heartsick because their father can't bother with them and scared that I'm trying to replace him."

She went to her desk and plopped down into her chair. Exhaustion, emotional and physical, overwhelmed her.

Ryder leaned his back against the lateral file cabinet. "What about his mother? Have you called her?"

"To tattle on him? I doubt he'd appreciate that."

"She might have some influence on him."

"Ruth and my relationship is tricky at best." Tatum shook her head. "She already suspects something between you and me. She might jump to the wrong conclusion."

"How could asking for her help in convincing Monty to visit his kids be misconstrued? It's to their benefit. And his. And hers, really."

"You're right." A less pleasant thought occurred to Tatum. "She might ask me to bring the kids to her house more often. Monty does visit her when he's in town." But not his own children. Tatum just didn't understand.

"Great," Ryder said. "Especially since I'll be moving to that same area."

"They might not like it. They're still afraid I'm going

to leave them with her again. Drew wouldn't go with her the day of the parade."

"What would it hurt to initiate a conversation with her?"

"Nothing, I suppose." Tatum conceded she could be making a mountain out of a molehill. "I'll call her tonight." She suddenly noticed a printout of the contract for Lynda Spencer on the corner of her desk and reached for it. "I finished drawing this up. It's ready for you and your father's review."

He took the contract, gave it a cursory once-over, then, grabbing the pen off her desk, signed on the bottom of the third page.

"You didn't even read it," she accused.

"Don't need to."

"Ryder. I'd feel a whole lot better if you and Mercer both looked at it."

"I was there when we, when you, negotiated the contract with Lynda. I'm well aware of the terms."

That was true. "Still."

"Send it." He promptly stood. "I have a meeting with Joe Blackwater. He's on his way here."

The rodeo promoter was one of the Becketts' oldest clients. He'd also been instrumental in helping to clear Deacon's name when he was falsely accused of causing a bull goring accident eleven years ago.

Tatum walked Ryder to the door. "See you later?"

"Depends on how long Joe wants to shoot the breeze and when you leave to pick up the kids."

"I'll call you after I talk to my mother-in-law."

"You'd better."

Hauling her into his arms, he planted a kiss on her mouth that sent a tingle clear to her toes.

She swayed unsteadily when he released her. "Wow. What was that for?"

"Putting those doubts of yours to rest."

His grin could be considered confident. Cocky, even. On him, it looked good.

She stood at the window after he left and watched him saunter across the open area to meet Joe Blackwater.

Ryder's kiss hadn't erased her doubts. Tatum was too practical for that. It had, however, lessened them. Ryder did have that effect on her.

Should she be worried? Probably. Tatum could easily lose her head around him, as she'd proven more than once.

Chapter Fourteen

Ryder and his father stopped at the Flat Iron for breakfast on their way to the arena. He shoveled his food into his mouth, only half listening to Mercer, his thoughts constantly straying to Tatum.

They were going out tonight. On a date. To Tony's Pizza Parlor for dinner, followed by dancing at the Hole in the Wall Saloon. Local spots where they were bound to be seen and recognized. Eventually, everyone would know they were dating, and Ryder had no problem with that.

Being with her, getting to know her, looking into her eyes and hanging on her every word, that was the important part. If their good-night kiss turned into more and they had a repeat of the other night, who was he to object? If not, that was okay with him. Ryder intended to take this relationship seriously and to make the most of it.

Her call to Ruth had netted some results. Monty phoned the kids, and, according to Tatum, they'd talked for a record-breaking thirty minutes. No plans, however, to visit. One step at a time, Ryder supposed.

Only when his father mentioned the bulls did Ryder perk up and pay attention.

"Mom finally caved?"

"I prefer to say she appreciates a deal when it comes along. That and we made a good haul on the Wild West Days Rodeo. Better than expected. We're going to the loan office today to sign the papers."

"Wow. That was fast."

"I told you, Harlo wasn't going to wait forever. I'm lucky he waited as long as he did." His father drained the last of his coffee. "If we want those bulls to pay for themselves, we're going to have to promote the heck out of the arena. You'll have your work cut out for you."

Ryder had planned to tell his family about Velocity Concept at the staff meeting this morning. Maybe it couldn't wait.

"Dad. I have some news."

"You're not still thinking of leaving." It wasn't a question.

"I've accepted a job at an ad agency in northwest Phoenix."

The explosion Ryder anticipated didn't happen. Instead, his father calmly asked, "How soon?"

"I told them I needed two weeks to wrap things up here before I could leave. That was yesterday."

There was a long, heavy pause. "Dammit, Ryder. Why?"

"I told you from the start my coming back was only temporary."

"A few weeks isn't temporary. It's a vacation. We need you."

"Tatum can help. She'd make a great assistant to you." He considered mentioning dating Tatum, then thought better of it.

"She's not family."

"Close enough." Ryder pushed his empty plate away. He had a lot to accomplish before the staff meeting at eleven. "We should probably get going."

"We aren't done talking about this. Just wait till your mother hears."

He was probably wasting his breath, but he tried anyway. "Dad. The decision's made."

His father shook his head. "It was our dream to—"

"Your dream. Not mine."

"Rodeoing's in your blood."

"But not in my heart."

"I'll give you a raise."

"Give Tatum the raise. She's going to deserve it before long. You'll see."

"Why do you keep pushing her?"

"What do you have against her?"

"She's an art teacher, for crying out loud. She'll quit us the first chance she gets."

Like me. His father didn't have to say it.

"She won't quit if you give her a reason to stay."

"It didn't work for you."

Ryder ignored the bite in his father's voice. "Give it a rest, will you?"

"Is this because you and your mother still aren't getting along?"

Would it make a difference if they were? "In all honesty, no."

"Don't you think it's time the two of you made up? The reasons for your anger at her aren't valid anymore."

"She didn't take you back, Dad. You had to wrangle your way in. To a business that was half yours to begin with. Forget the astronomical amount of money she owed you. Still owes you."

"I don't care about the money."

Ryder didn't let go. "If not for Liberty tracking you down, neither of us would be here. Just because we are doesn't excuse what she did."

"What if I asked you to make peace with her? For me."

Saying no to his father had never been easy for Ryder. "I'll think about it."

"That's all I ask." His father grabbed his key ring and wallet off the table. "I'll get the tab."

At the arena, the two of them separated. While his father went to the office—it was his habit to tackle paperwork early—Ryder took his camcorder to the bull pens. Whenever he had a few spare minutes, he'd been taking footage and was almost ready to forward it to his friend for editing. Hopefully, the final digital short would be ready in time to promote their next rodeo. It would be something special to leave his family.

He was almost done when his name was spoken softly behind him, in a way he hadn't heard in years. Shutting off the camcorder, he turned and faced his mother. Honestly, he'd been half expecting her. News traveled quickly among his family. His father had probably gone straight to Sunny after their heated exchange.

Ryder didn't mince words. "I take it Dad told you about the job."

"He did."

"If you're here to try and change my mind, don't bother."

She didn't so much as flinch at his harsh tone. "I understood why you left when you were a boy. You and Mercer were close as could be. Had the kind of father-son relationship every mother hopes for, and you missed him terribly. Blamed me for the divorce. I was certain after a few months, or maybe even a year, that you'd tire of your father's drinking, miss me and Cassidy, your friends, and come home. Only you didn't. Other than those few summers during high school." She searched his face, her expression pensive. "Why, Ryder?"

"I might have. If you'd have shown even the slightest decency to Dad. He did stop drinking. Right after I moved in with him."

"Yes, but there were no guarantees he wouldn't start again, and I couldn't take the chance. I loved him too much."

"Loved him? You had a funny way of showing it."

"I knew as long as he and I remained married, he wouldn't change. In large part because I enabled him. I thought, hoped, that by divorcing him, the shock would force him to get sober. Maybe even before we actually went through with it. Losing me sobered him up once before."

"What do you mean, before?"

"Your father was a wild one when we first dated. I thought he just liked to party with the boys and drink too much. I might have been young and inexperienced, but, after a while, even I could see that he had a drinking problem. I insisted he stop or we were through."

"And he did?"

"Didn't touch a single drop." Her eyes filled with sadness. "Then, he started again at your grandfather's wake and, this time, didn't stop. Nothing I said or did made a difference. Eventually, alcohol replaced everything important in his life. His job, his family, his friends. Me."

"I'm sorry, Mom, but I just don't remember any of that."

"Oh, he was an expert at hiding it from you and Cassidy. When you two were anywhere near, he was the epitome of a fun and happy dad, even if he was tanked. When you weren't, he became bitter and morose and angry. Really angry. The fights were the worst."

"With you?"

"With everyone. Sometimes, it was like a switch was flipped. One minute, he was laughing and joking. The next, he was accusing whomever of some invented infraction that generally resulted in a brawl. Three times in three months I was called to the clinic when he was hurt. Twice, I had to bail him out of jail."

Jail? Ryder hadn't heard these stories before. "Did he ever hurt you?"

"Not physically," she assured him. "Not ever."

"I didn't know."

"I didn't want you to know. Or your sister."

"I might have been able to help."

"I doubt that." She gave him a sad smile. "There were nights he didn't come home, and I'm not kidding when I tell you I was glad for the reprieve. I had my hands full as it was, taking care of you kids and running the arena. I didn't need a drunk to nurse on top of that."

"Did you ever try to get him help? AA. Counseling."

"Countless times. That's the thing about an addict, no one can help them if they won't help themselves. All I could do was try my best to keep the business from going under and to provide for the family."

Ryder realized with more than a little guilt that he hadn't ever considered how hard it must have been for his mother. Hadn't cared enough to ask. He'd been too busy being angry at her.

"I might have stuck it out a whole lot longer, even when he lost all that money on a herd of sick calves." Her voice shook. "It was the accident with Cassidy that convinced me he had to leave. I couldn't forgive him for that. Or take the chance that something worse might happen the next time. My children came first. Even at the expense of my husband and marriage. I know that's difficult for you to comprehend."

"Not as much as you'd think."

Before coming home to Reckless, Ryder wouldn't have given his mother's argument much weight. Meeting Tatum, seeing her relentless devotion to her children, had altered his perspective. Like his mother, she'd endured hardship and sacrificed greatly for the sake of her kids. Also like his mother, she was dealing with a daughter who sorely missed her father and didn't understand why he had to go away.

If Ryder could be understanding and sympathetic to her, could he not grant his mother some of the same understanding and sympathy? It was something to consider.

"You free later?" He held up the camcorder. "I'll be done here in about fifteen minutes."

She hesitated, perhaps unsure why he was asking. "I have to run to the bank before the staff meeting."

"Later, then? I'd like to continue this conversation." A delighted smile illuminated her face. "I'd like that, too."

"We still have a lot of ground to cover, Mom."

"One step at a time, sweetheart."

He gave her a one-armed hug that was filled with far more emotion than the full embrace they'd shared his first day home.

She reached up to pat his cheek. "I can't help myself," she said by way of apology.

"I don't mind." And he didn't.

"See you." She left, a spring to her step he hadn't seen before today. Ryder chuckled. They hadn't mended all their broken bridges, but they'd made a start. And it felt good.

He was just finishing filming when his cell phone chimed. He read the display and groaned. His father? Really? The man couldn't walk out and find him?

"What's up, Dad?"

"I need to see you right away. I'm in the office."

The curt demand rubbed Ryder the wrong way. He felt six rather than thirty-six. "I'll be done in about fifteen minutes."

"Now, Ryder. It's important. You need to see this."

"All right. Fine." He powered down the camcorder and returned it to the case.

Tatum was sitting at her desk when he entered. He'd have liked to give her a kiss, but that would be entirely inappropriate, and he'd had enough trouble in the past with something far less provocative than a kiss.

"Morning." He flashed her a smile as he passed her desk.

"Hey." The smile she gave him in return was ripe with promise for the coming evening.

Ryder suppressed a groan. Surviving the long day wasn't going to be easy. He'd be counting the minutes until he picked her up tonight.

"Shut the door," his father said upon seeing him, his tone brusque.

Ryder drew up short. "What's wrong?"

"Now."

He did as his father insisted, his defenses rising.

"Sit." When Ryder complied, his father handed him a thin sheaf of papers.

He scanned the first page of the contract for Lynda Spencer. "Yeah?" He started to hand the papers back.

"Dammit to hell, Ryder."

"What's wrong?"

"How could you agree to these terms?"

"They're good."

"They're ridiculous."

Ryder flipped to the second page where the terms were outlined and read. "Wait," he muttered. "These aren't right."

"You can say that again."

"There must be a mistake." He saw it then, a transposition—numbers reversed—and his blood ran cold.

"You said Tatum handled the meeting and negotiated the terms."

"She did, but this isn't what we agreed to."

"I spoke to Lynda Spencer before I called you. Frankly, she's pretty happy, which is why she signed the contract and returned it so fast."

"She can't expect us to uphold these terms."

"It's a done deal."

"We'll go back to her—"

"Forget it. That's not how your mother and I do business. We have a reputation to uphold, and honor our contracts even when we've screwed up."

"I understand that, Dad."

"We can't have an employee working for us who makes mistakes that cost us thousands of dollars."

"You're not firing Tatum."

"She sure isn't getting any promotion."

"This is my fault entirely. She asked me to review the contract. Even handed it to me, in fact. I signed it without looking and instructed her to send it."

His father stared at him as if he'd just announced his

intentions to run for president. "What in God's name is the matter with you? You let a complete novice negotiate a contract with an important new client and then send it out unreviewed. I can't believe what I'm hearing. How did you ever make it to head marketing executive?"

The verbal lashing was harsh. And deserved.

Ryder's head pounded. He'd been here before. Not with his father but in a meeting at Madison-Monroe. Then, his boss had asked almost the identical question. Ryder hadn't had a good answer that time, either.

Blurring the boundary between business and personal. Hadn't he learned his lesson already?

"I'll call Lynda," Ryder said. "Explain the situation. Make it right."

"Weren't you listening? This contract is signed by both parties. Legal and binding. We are officially screwed."

"Take the money out of my salary."

His father continued as if he hadn't heard Ryder. "There go the funds for transporting the new bulls."

"I'll run by the bank in town and withdraw the money now." He could borrow against his credit card.

"Don't you think instead you should stay here and clean up this mess?"

"I said I'll pay you back."

"I don't want your money."

"No, you just want to control me. Use what happened to strong-arm me into staying." It was the same tactic his father had employed on Liberty, Cassidy and their mother. They'd resisted. And despite being in the wrong, Ryder was resisting, too.

"You're missing the point," his father said. "You have an obligation to your family."

"I have an obligation to rectify my wrongs. And I will. But I'm still taking that job, Dad." He stood. "And leaving Reckless."

His father's features darkened. "Send Tatum in on your way out."

"You aren't talking to her without Mom present."

"I'm her boss."

"You're angry at me. Don't take it out on her."

"I'm just going to talk to her."

"It was a typo. One I should have caught when I reviewed the contract—which I didn't. She followed instructions."

"A typo, as you call it, is a careless oversight. She should have double-checked her work before giving it to you."

"And that's what you're going to talk to her about," Ryder stated. "Double-checking her work. With Mom present," he reiterated.

"She's gone. Won't be back until the staff meeting. This can't wait."

"Then you talk to Tatum with me present."

"You're making more out of this than you need to."

"You shouldn't be alone with Tatum. It's bad policy."

"Policy?"

"You want to avoid any misunderstandings. It's less likely to happen with a third person in the room." If only Ryder had heeded his own advice.

His father frowned. "Are you saying she could accuse me of something I didn't do?"

"Or something you didn't say. People often react badly when they're being reprimanded. They're upset. Not listening. Misinterpreting. Better to wait for Mom."

He didn't believe Tatum was like his former coworker, exaggerating a situation for her own personal agenda. His suggestion was also to protect Tatum. She needed an advocate, and his mother would fill that role.

"Okay." His father leaned back in his chair. "I'll wait."

Ryder expelled a long breath. He wanted to be in on the meeting. He also knew from experience that wasn't wise.

"You and I aren't through," his father added.

They would talk again, and when they did, Ryder would be handing his father the money this mistake had cost the arena.

"I'll be back in an hour."

His father's gaze pinned him in place. "Don't say a word to her. You hear me? I know you two have a thing."

"I won't."

As much as Ryder wanted to give Tatum a heads-up, he'd keep his mouth shut. Every move he made, every step he took, from this moment on had to be carefully executed. He wouldn't endanger Tatum's job any more than it already was.

In the outer office, he paused at her desk.

"Everything okay?" she asked.

"Great."

"Ryder."

"I'll catch you later." Because she needed reassurance, he squeezed her shoulder.

"Okay. But I'm—"

"I promise you, everything will be fine."

It would be, too. He'd move heaven and earth if necessary to safeguard her. And if his father dared to fire her, he'd help her fight it tooth and nail.

Once outside, Ryder went straight to his truck. How could he be so stupid? Twice in three months he'd made a colossal error. Twice he'd let his feelings for a woman affect his better judgment.

Only this time, he wasn't the only one to suffer the consequences. He'd cost his family a sizeable amount of money and brought the woman he truly cared about under unnecessary scrutiny.

TATUM DIDN'T PHONE Ryder after her meeting with Mercer and Sunny. Instead, she placed a call to a temporary agency she'd applied to right after losing her teaching job. The Becketts had come through with the office manager position, so she hadn't followed up with the agency. She did this afternoon.

They had a position open at a preschool in Mesa. She could start next week as soon as she passed the background check and completed the application process. Tatum requested twenty-four hours to think about it. There were the Becketts to consider; she owed them a reasonable notice. And there were her art classes. Her students' parents deserved reasonable notice, too, and any refunds due.

The meeting with Sunny and Mercer had been her worst nightmare come true. For two hours after Ryder left, she'd fretted and stewed, sensing something had happened between him and his father. Or, that he'd told his family about the job offer, and there'd been a falling-out.

Never in her wildest imagination had she thought she'd made an error in the Spencer contract or that she would be receiving a stern reprimand.

Sunny had assured her the oversight was an honest one and that ultimate responsibility lay with Ryder. Tatum took only a small amount of consolation from that. Yes, he should have reviewed the contract. She'd asked him to do it. But the actual transposition was her carelessness.

She wasn't normally like that. Tatum took pride in her work, always did her best. She was organized and diligent and paid attention to details. Except for the Lynda Spencer contract.

Then, she'd allowed blind determination and Ryder's overconfidence in her abilities to cloud her judgment. She should have refused his directive and not sent out the contract until it was reviewed. By Mercer if not Ryder. But she'd been pleased and flattered and lulled by the pretty picture of the future Ryder had painted and a desire to be worthy of his affections. Such a fool!

God, what would her mother-in-law say when she found out? Tatum's stomach twisted into an uncomfortable knot. Ruth would probably try and gain custody of the kids through Monty, claiming Tatum wasn't in a financially secure enough position to adequately provide for them. She might be right, considering that Tatum had been in this exact same position six short months ago.

Knowing Sunny and Cassidy were having dinner right about now, Tatum pulled into the driveway and unloaded her kids from the car. With Adam balanced on her hip and the other two in tow, she knocked on the Becketts' back door. Cassidy answered it.

"Hi. You're a little early."

The plan had been for Cassidy and Sunny to watch the kids while Tatum and Ryder went on their date. She'd explained the change in plans to her children on the drive over. They weren't happy to be missing out on playtime with their friend.

What would Ryder think when he showed up at her place and she wasn't there? What would he think when he called her cell and she didn't answer because she'd purposefully left it in the car? Doubtless he'd be unhappy, too.

"Sorry to interrupt you at dinnertime," Tatum said, "but do you have a minute?"

Concern clouded Cassidy's features. The door swung wide. "Sure, sure. Of course."

Drew tumbled in first. "Where's Benjie?"

"Watching TV with my mom." Cassidy gave him a gentle nudge. "Go on, if you want."

He tore across the kitchen and around the corner. Gretchen also went, at a considerably more sedate pace. Adam, evidently having another one of his "off days"—that, or he'd picked up on Tatum's state of mind—clung to her and whined softly.

She watched until both older children disappeared, thinking Drew's hair was in dire need of a cut. She should have taken him to the barber last weekend, only she'd been too preoccupied with Ryder and the mock wedding. A lot of things had gone unattended recently, and she was paying for it now. Well, after tonight, she'd be able to catch up.

"Can I talk to your mom, too?" Tatum asked. "I won't take long."

In response, Cassidy turned off the oven and lowered the heat beneath a simmering pot. "Be right back."

She took the same route as Drew and Gretchen. A minute later, she returned with Sunny. The two must have exchanged words, for Sunny wore the same worried expression as Cassidy.

"Honey, about today," Sunny said, "I know you're upset. Mercer was much too hard on you."

"He wasn't. He was doing his job." Tatum squared her shoulders as much as possible with Adam in her arms. "I came here tonight to tender my resignation."

"No!" Cassidy rushed forward. "You are not quitting. It was a stupid little whoops. I make them all the time."

"It's not just the Spencer contract and the numbers mixup. It's the reason I made the mistake in the first place." Ignoring the painful lump in her throat, she shifted Adam to her other hip. "I let my personal life interfere with my job. Affect my judgment. That's unprofessional and unacceptable."

"This is about Ryder, then," Cassidy said, her voice flat.

"It's about me. I love you both, even more because you came through for me and the kids when I really needed it. But we all know teaching and art are my first loves, and I'm not an office manager."

"You're a great office manager."

"I'm competent. Good on my best days. But I'm no administrative assistant, and I'm certainly no marketing or promotion person."

"You don't have to be," Sunny insisted.

"The customers adore you," Cassidy added.

"And I like them. Interacting with customers has been the best part of working here."

"Then, stay."

Tatum wanted Sunny and Cassidy to understand and did her best to explain. "All the years I spent teaching, I was careful to never cross the line. And it was difficult sometimes, believe you me. The students with issues, the parents who didn't care, I often wished I could put those lines aside, but I didn't. Four months on this job and I not only do that, I cost you a substantial amount of money."

"We'll recover," Sunny assured her. "We have before. From much worse."

"Please reconsider," Cassidy pleaded. "Mom's right. A few thousand dollars isn't that big of a deal."

A few thousand dollars? Tatum thought about what she could do with that sum. Put a deposit down on a rental house. Finally get those new tires for her car. Start a college fund for her children.

"It's for the best," she said. "I can't continue working here with Ryder."

"He's leaving." Cassidy sounded as if she'd been expecting her brother's departure all along.

"I heard."

"Then, why quit?"

"You've been good to me. Better than I deserve. I refuse to be a hindrance."

Funny, Ryder said essentially the same thing about his job with the arena only on a temporary basis. Were they both taking advantage of their loved ones? She hadn't understood his reasons for seeking a different job before. Now, they were crystal clear.

"You are not a hindrance," Sunny insisted.

"I went from living with my parents to living with Monty. Other than the twenty months since the divorce, and not counting the two months we stayed here with you, I haven't lived on my own. I wouldn't be now if not for you. It's time I grew up. Stopped depending on others to carry my load."

"Tatum." Sunny looked as if her heart was breaking.

"It's obvious I can't rely on Monty, other than for child support. Even when his children were at risk of losing the only home they'd ever known, he didn't step up. I have to make it on my own, or as much as I can."

"What are you going to do?" Cassidy asked, tears threatening to fall.

Adam had begun to drift off. Tatum patted his back while rocking from side to side. "I have a potential teaching job in Mesa. At a preschool. Temporary to start, but it could work into a permanent position. I'd have to begin next week. I know it's short notice…"

"No worries," Sunny insisted. "We'll manage."

"What about the art classes?" Cassidy asked. "Can you turn those into something full-time?"

"I doubt it. There aren't enough children in Reckless interested in learning to paint."

"I'll speak to the board members," Sunny offered. "Maybe we can shift some money around. Or, you could substitute teach."

"Don't bother. You'd be wasting your time." Tatum had no expectations that the board would change their position. Not without a new source of revenue.

"Have you told Ryder yet?" Sunny asked. Both she and Cassidy knew about his and Tatum's date.

"I will."

"When?"

"I'm not sure. Maybe tonight."

"He feels terrible." Sunny said. "And blames himself.

Ah, so he'd talked with Sunny, not just Mercer. Tatum admitted to being curious how that conversation went.

"He shouldn't."

"Yes, he should." Cassidy huffed with indignation. "It was his responsibility to review that contract before you sent it out."

Sadness filled Tatum. "You're always so hard on him. And Mercer. They're family, and you only get one."

Cassidy looked chagrined. "You're right."

Tatum thought of Monty and Ruth. Was she too hard on them, as well? They were still family. Her children's father and grandmother. Perhaps Tatum should heed her own advice.

All at once, Benjie appeared in the kitchen. Sliding to a stop in his stockinged feet, he announced that he was starving. Tatum took her cue to leave.

"Come on, kids," she hollered. "Time to hit the road."

Her small troupe responded, heads hanging as if leaving was the worst punishment ever rendered in the entire history of the world.

Tatum checked her phone after getting into the car. Three missed calls from Ryder. A small icon appeared at the top of her phone's display, alerting her she had a voice-mail message. Maybe more than one.

She didn't call Ryder on the drive home, preferring privacy when they spoke. Holding her breath in anticipation, she pulled into her parking space at her apartment complex. Would he be there waiting for her? As it turned out, he wasn't. She was both relieved and disappointed.

Thirty minutes later, she answered his next phone call. He didn't bother with hello. "Are you okay?"

"I'm fine. Adam, though, is sick. I think he's running a fever. Sorry, I should have phoned."

A fib, yes. But Tatum just couldn't face Ryder tonight. Not after the day she'd had.

"Can I help?"

"I'm just putting him to bed now." That much was true. "Sorry about tonight."

"I could come over."

The tenderness in his voice tore at her already vulnerable heart. "It's not a good time. I'm tired." Another truth.

"Okay. I'll call you in the morning." The tenderness had vanished. He'd figured out she was blowing him off.

She hated herself in this moment. She'd hate herself worse when they finally did talk, and she told him about her decision to quit the arena and leave Reckless.

Ryder would probably hate her, too.

Chapter Fifteen

Ryder found Tatum in the Ship-With-Ease Store, speaking with Lenny Faust. He'd tracked her there after learning that she'd given her notice.

Her notice! What the heck was she thinking, quitting the Easy Money and moving? The anger he felt, at himself, his family, his father especially, at her even, was overshadowed by his fear that she might actually leave Reckless, going who knew where, and it was all his fault.

Cassidy had let the news slip earlier, assuming Tatum had already told him about her termination. Later, he'd have to apologize to his sister for his outburst. At the moment, finding Tatum and convincing her not to quit took precedence. Clearly, she'd had a knee-jerk reaction to the reprimand she'd received and wasn't looking at the long term.

A buzzer announced his arrival at the store. Tatum stood at the counter, Lenny on the other side facing her. They both turned to stare at him. Lenny winked. Tatum remained stoic. Ryder cut a direct path to Tatum. "Can we talk?"

"Give me a few minutes." She held herself rigid.

"Take your time," Lenny said and hooked his thumb over his shoulder. "I've got some cartons in the storeroom to unpack."

Ryder barely waited for the other man to leave. "You *quit*."

"We are *not* having this discussion here."

"I agree."

He took her by the arm and, ignoring her small gasp of

protest, led her to the art studio next door. Lenny might be in the storeroom, but the walls weren't soundproof, and Ryder wanted to keep his and Tatum's conversation away from prying ears.

"You can't," he said the instant they were behind the closed door. "You need this job."

"I have another one lined up."

"What? Where?"

She raised her chin a notch. "It's not really any of your business."

"The hell it isn't. We're dating."

"Technically, we haven't been on even one date."

Her remark hit him in the gut, stronger than any fist. "Did the other night mean that little to you?"

Her features crumpled. "It meant more to me than you can know."

"Not enough, apparently, because you're hightailing it out of here the second we hit a bump in the road."

"This is more than a bump, Ryder."

"You were reprimanded. For a mistake that wasn't your fault. Big deal. It happens all the time. You learn, make changes and have it out with your boss if necessary. Hardly a reason to blow off your job and pull up stakes. Move your entire family."

Now it was her turn to react. "It is a big deal. I cost the Easy Money a lot of money."

"I cost them the money. I'm trying to repay it, but, so far, my parents won't let me. I'm thinking of just depositing the money directly into the arena bank account."

"I won't let you! It's, it's—"

"My decision. And I'd do a lot more than that if it stopped you from leaving. You love living in Reckless. And you like your job at the arena."

"You can't simply buy your way out of this."

"I'm making recompense for my error."

"Not your error. Mine."

He was growing weary of her stubbornness. "We can argue this point until we're both blue in the face. It's not the real issue. Your quitting is. You're upset and you're also embarrassed."

Her blush confirmed it.

"Take a day and calm down."

The blush morphed into a flush of anger. "You just don't get it. How come you can quit your job and move away when you screw up but not me?"

"My mistake was a lot bigger. And could have cost my employer considerably more than a few thousand dollars. Yours was a typo."

"It's *exactly* the same. I allowed my relationship with a coworker to affect my judgment and cost the company. The amount is irrelevant."

He wasn't ready to concede. "I was pressured into re-signing rather than face a potential lawsuit, and your employer wants you to stay. In fact, they're heartbroken you quit." He recalled Cassidy's sobs when she'd told him about Tatum's notice.

"Not your father."

"He likes you."

"I'm not his first choice for an office manager, and he sure as heck doesn't want me handling any of the marketing or promotion. With good reason."

Frankly, she baffled Ryder sometimes with her mulishness. "You're still stuck on the notion that my family is giving you charity."

"They have. Do you think somebody else would get a mere slap on the wrist? I've been treated differently from the beginning."

"Me, too. And my sisters. We're family."

"Dammit, Ryder. You aren't making this easy."

"I'm trying not to."

She groaned with frustration. "It's time for me to grow up. Other than going to college and obtaining my teaching degree, I haven't done one responsible adult thing on my own. When Monty left me, I mismanaged my finances and lost my house."

"He should have helped you. He had a responsibility."

"Maybe. Or maybe I simply messed up. I may resent my mother-in-law, but without her, I'm not sure what I would have done. Now, I've messed up again. I want to learn my lessons, handle my problems, and I can't do that if I continually let other people rescue me."

The part of his brain that remained rational saw the logic behind her argument. It gave him pause and cleared his head.

"Okay. Fine. Quit the arena. But that's no reason to leave Reckless."

"I need a job. There aren't many in town for the taking. Not that would enable me to earn a decent living."

He asked the question in a much more reasonable tone. "Where are you going?"

"Mesa."

His shoulders slumped, the fight going out of him. All this anger and frustration for nothing. Mesa was an hour at most from north Phoenix where he'd be located. In fact, now that he thought about it, the distance was more doable than her living in Reckless. He'd been wrong to jump to conclusions. To come in with both guns blazing. Really wrong.

"I'll help you move," he said.

"I beg your pardon."

"We can do it together. Look for new places. Buy furniture. I've got a bunch of stuff in storage." An idea occurred to him. A good one. "Let's rent a place together. Halfway between our two jobs. There'd be some driving for both of us, but later we could buy a house, and you could look for a closer job."

"What the heck are you doing?" She glared at him, furious. "I'm not moving in with you."

"Why?" The idea made complete sense to him.

"Weren't you listening to me? Because I need to grow up, Ryder."

"This isn't charity. It's two people in a relationship planning a life together. A future."

"I have to think of my children."

"They like me."

"Not Gretchen."

"She'll come around."

"How well you get along with them isn't the problem. I'm just not ready to make any kind of commitment. Not until I figure out my life."

The slam to the gut Ryder received earlier was nothing compared to this. He felt pummeled, as if he'd been run over by a convoy of tanks.

He could love Tatum. Might already be in love with her. Yet, she was tossing him aside like yesterday's garbage.

How wrong he'd been, and how right she'd been when she'd said she wasn't ready for a relationship.

"Look." As if sensing his anguish, she made an appeal. "We can still see each other."

At that, Ryder laughed. A loud, short burst that had her taking a step back. "See each other?" He'd stupidly believed he meant more to her than that.

"I wasn't being funny."

"No, you weren't."

He was vaguely aware that his remarks had wounded her, but he didn't care. She'd shot her share of arrows without thought or concern.

"And now that I want to take our relationship to the next level, you're the one putting on the brakes. Tell me that isn't funny."

Sweeping her hair over her shoulder with a jerk of her hand, she started for the door. "I think I should go."

Ryder didn't stop her, which seemed to give her second thoughts because she hesitated at the door leading to the store, her hand on the knob, a perplexed expression on her face.

"That's it?" she asked.

"What else is there?" He didn't try to mask the bitterness in his voice. "You've decided. Any arguments I make will fall on deaf ears."

Pain ravaged her face. "This isn't how I wanted it to end."

"At least you're admitting you wanted it to end."

"Not true," she protested. "You're twisting my words."

"Am I? Or, are you finally being completely honest, with yourself and me?"

At that, she turned the doorknob and left, walking out of the studio and out of his life forever. He waited a full two minutes before letting the emotional weight of what had just transpired push him down into the depths of emotional despair.

How he made it to his truck he wasn't sure. Where he was heading, he had no idea.

At the street light, he stopped and let the truck idle, not proceeding even when the light turned green until the driver behind him laid on the horn.

Just as well he was leaving Reckless. After today, there was no reason for him to stay.

"You're wrong."

Ryder cranked his head in the direction of his father's voice. "About what?" Frankly, he could take his pick of accusations.

"With Tatum."

He'd expected his mother to be the one giving him grief, not his father—who'd often treated Tatum with ambivalence. Yet, there Mercer stood at the door to the guest bedroom Ryder had occupied since returning to Reckless, a disgusted scowl on his whiskered face.

"Your mother called." His father didn't wait for an invitation, not that Ryder would have issued one, and entered the bedroom. "She said Tatum is upset."

"That was some reprimand you gave her. She did quit."

"Damn woman is overly sensitive, if you ask me." His father grumbled something unintelligible under his breath. "But that's not why she's leaving Reckless."

"She told me differently." Five days ago, to be specific.

"You disappointed her."

Ryder turned from the window he'd been staring out of, mentally reviewing his list of regrets. "How exactly did I do that? By wanting to date?"

"You pushed her into taking a responsibility she wasn't ready for and didn't want."

"No kidding." His father had some nerve. "I seem to remember telling you the exact same thing before you decided to reprimand her and not me."

At that moment, Ryder felt the need to haul his suitcase out of the closet and start packing. He was heading to Phoenix this weekend in search of an apartment near his new job.

His father stared at the suitcase. "I thought you were giving us two weeks' notice."

"I figured since I'm such a washout, you'd have no objections to me cutting that short."

"You're wrong."

Ryder shook his head and threw the suitcase on to the bed with enough force, the headboard banged the wall.

"Fix this," his father said.

"The wall?"

"Don't be stupid. You know what I'm talking about. Convince Tatum to stay."

"I thought you wanted her gone."

"Hell, no, I don't want her gone. And not just because it would break your mother's heart and quite possibly cost me my relationship with Cassidy."

"Then, why?"

"I didn't want her doing your job, making it easier for you to leave. She was, is, a fine office manager."

"You keep forgetting, I never intended to stay permanently."

"Because you don't like taking handouts from your family?"

That sounded a lot like Tatum's complaint. Why had he insisted she wasn't taking charity from his family and shouldn't resent their help when he felt the same way? If he examined his reasons more closely, he probably wouldn't like what he found. He'd been out for himself and willing to use Tatum and her personal plight to get what he wanted.

She was right to toss him aside. He didn't deserve her.

Come to think of it, he didn't deserve his family, either. They'd been nothing but good to him these past weeks. Best to make a clean break, painful though it might be.

"Look, I like working at the arena. But the fact is, I have more potential. Greater ambitions. And you're overpaying me."

"Well." Despite them being the same height, his father managed to look down his nose at Ryder. "Didn't realize we were such a step down for you."

"That didn't come out right."

"No? Somehow I think it came out exactly how you intended."

"You're right." Ryder should apologize.

Rather than lash out in anger, his father sat on the footlocker at the end of the bed. "I did the same thing when I left all those years ago. I pretty much hated myself and figured other people felt the same. If they didn't, I was bound and determined they would by the time I left. Worked hard at it, too. Like you're doing."

Ryder really didn't appreciate how well his father knew him.

"Let's say, for the sake of argument, you're capable of more than the Easy Money has to offer. When did you get so all-fire full of yourself that you stopped having to make the most of a job and have everything handed to you on a silver platter?"

The remark struck Ryder like a blast of cold water. He'd worked his butt off for the first dozen years of his career, turning a sometimes mediocre position into an exciting and rewarding one. Had the fiasco at Madison-Monroe altered him? Taken the wind from his sails? The thought that it had rankled him.

"I might not have given this job a fair shake."

"How 'bout that?" His father chuckled dryly. "Your old man isn't as dumb as you thought."

"I never said you were dumb." The suitcase remained open and empty on the bed. Ryder had yet to throw any clothes in it.

"Can't say the same about you." Mercer shook his head.

"Because I'm leaving?" Why did they have to argue the same point over and over?

"Because you're letting that pretty young woman walk out on you."

That hit a nerve. "I asked her to stay. Suggested we rent a place together."

"Moving a little fast, aren't you?"

"Doesn't matter. She won't listen to reason."

"Maybe the problem is you're not being reasonable. Women think differently than men."

"Like you're an expert on women," Ryder scoffed.

"Trust me, I'm the furthest thing from an expert. But I don't need to be one to know you should go after Tatum. Fight for her. I didn't when your mother divorced me. Took me twenty-five years to come to my senses. Even then, I needed Liberty to show me the error of my ways. I'm trying to save you the trouble."

"Dad—"

"Not sure what went wrong at that last job of yours and, frankly, I don't care. But whatever happened changed you.

You're not the same man I knew a few months ago. You're whipped."

Whipped? Ryder hated the sound of that. It too closely resembled what he'd been thinking himself.

"I got involved with a coworker. It didn't end well. She made trouble for me. A lot of trouble. She did it because I let her."

"Doesn't sound like anything Tatum would do."

"No, I'm the one who made trouble for her."

"Look." His father stood and put himself between Ryder and the suitcase on the bed. "You can fix this. There's still time."

"And I presume you're going to tell me how."

"Chase Tatum down. Convince her you love her and will do anything for her and those kids of hers. Who desperately need a father, from what I can tell. Make her stay. Propose if you have to."

"Propose? Didn't you just say it was too soon to move in together? Now you're suggesting I propose?"

"Women want a commitment. Living together is a token effort at best. No wonder she turned you down."

Hard to believe but his father did make sense. Ryder had known all along Tatum was the marrying kind, not the date-then-live-together kind.

"You could do worse than her."

"Truthfully, I'm not sure I could do any better. She's an amazing woman."

"Marriage isn't so bad," his father said. "In fact, I'm considering giving the honorable institution another shot."

Ryder did a double take. "You've met someone?"

"Gawd almighty, you really aren't very bright." Mercer shook his head in disgust. "I'm talking about your mother."

"She know about this?"

"Not yet. I'm waiting for the right moment to pop the question."

Ryder was thinking the right moment might be when

hell froze over, given his mother's resistance. But then, she had relented about purchasing the new bulls. And Liberty had told him she'd caught them kissing once outside the arena. Perhaps his father was more persuasive than Ryder gave him credit for.

"You sure you want to live the rest of your life wondering if you made the right decision? Or the wrong one?"

"She's dead set against reconciling. I've tried. She shuts me down every time." The past five days had been difficult for him. A living hell. He wasn't ready to repeat them.

"Charm her."

"Not that easy. She'd have to speak to me first."

"If you can't get her to talk to you, guess you're not the hotshot marketing exec you think you are."

"Not the same thing."

"I disagree. You give that gal your best sales pitch. The most important one you've ever made. See if she doesn't come around."

In a strange way, his father made sense. "And if she says no?"

"What if she says yes?"

Then Ryder would spend the rest of his life making her happy.

His father's next words spurred Ryder into action. "Get after it, son. Daylight's burning."

He left without a backward glance, hopped in his truck and drove to town, taking side roads to shave a few minutes off his time. On the way to Tatum's apartment, he ignored his father's earlier directive and placed a call to Lynda Spencer. The more he thought about it, the more determined he was to see if anything could be done about the contract fiasco.

She answered on the second ring. "Hello, Ryder."

"Do you have a minute?"

"Absolutely."

"About the contract."

"I was wondering when you were going to call me."

"There was a mistake. Numbers transposed."

"I saw that."

"We're going to honor the terms. You can count on us."

Surprise tinged her voice. "I appreciate that. Another contractor wouldn't."

"We both know you're getting a smoking deal."

"I agree. But what do you want, Ryder, if not to ask me to renegotiate the contract?"

He was a little disappointed she didn't offer to make the terms right. They had, after all, reached a verbal agreement. Having no choice, he plowed ahead.

"Give us your next six rodeos. For the same terms we originally agreed to at the restaurant. You owe us that much."

There was a moment of silence before she answered, "That's two years out. We don't normally contract more than a year in advance."

"We just purchased ten new bulls. From Harlo Billings." She'd recognize the name and the stellar reputation attached to it.

There was another lengthy pause. Ryder swore he could hear the wheels in Lynda's mind spinning.

Finally, she answered, "Done. I'll have a letter of intent drawn up and forwarded to your office."

Ryder allowed himself a smile. It would take two rodeos for the Becketts to recover the money they'd lost. The remaining four would be at a respectable profit. And they could use Lynda to promote even more new business.

He disconnected after saying goodbye, satisfaction coursing through him. He'd done his job, maybe for the first time since returning to Reckless. This was why his father had wanted him to work for the family. What he'd meant when he challenged Ryder to turn his position at the arena into all it could be.

Was that what he wanted? To stay in Reckless? Maybe.

Yes. But only on the condition he could convince Tatum to stay with him.

Ryder picked up his discarded cell phone and placed another call. This one to Myra. He knew from past experience that he worked best when under pressure and with the right motivation. If he had any chance of changing Tatum's mind, he needed to be sweating bullets.

"Hello, Ryder." Myra sounded glad to hear from him. After he told her the reason for his call, her demeanor noticeably cooled.

"Are you absolutely sure? This is an amazing opportunity."

For her, too. She stood to lose a substantial fee.

"I'm going to stay in Reckless. I haven't given the job with my family a fair shot." He went on to apologize for inconveniencing her and wasting her time. Ryder prided himself on following through with his commitments, and it bothered him to renege on this one.

"I have a couple associates looking for a change," he said. "I'll send them your way."

"Sure. Whatever."

He was offering her scraps at best, and she didn't hide her disappointment. Ryder decided he'd send her the money his parents refused to accept.

In front of Tatum's apartment, he pulled to a stop and parked along the curb. The tidy white triplex gleamed shiny in the afternoon light. Tatum's unit was on the east side. He hadn't noticed the painted flowerpots in the front with their white-and-yellow chrysanthemums when he'd been here the other night. Or the rooster lawn ornaments, frilly curtains visible in the front window and tire swing hanging from a tree in the front yard.

She'd done a lot to make the apartment, such as it was, an attractive home. Imagine what she could do to a real house. Ryder had always lived in a bachelor pad, devoid of a woman's touch. Before now, he hadn't thought he'd missed it. Before now, he hadn't known Tatum.

His brisk knock at her front door went unanswered, as did an insistent ringing of the doorbell. Where was she? When was she returning?

Ryder jogged to his truck. Odds were, she'd driven in to town. Either to pick up the boys from day care or to run errands.

He'd found her once before. He'd do it again. And, this time, he wouldn't let her go. Not until she'd listened to him.

Chapter Sixteen

"Where are we going, Mommy?"

"I have to stop by the store and talk to Mr. Faust."

Tatum dreaded this meeting with Lenny. By her estimation, and after a thorough and discouraging study of her finances the previous night, she could squeak by for about a month. That would give her enough time to finish out the remaining week of her two-week notice at the arena *and* earn enough money for a deposit and first month's rent on an apartment in Mesa.

Her mother-in-law wasn't happy. She wanted Tatum to locate closer to her. Actually, she'd wanted the kids to move back in with her. Just until Tatum was settled. So she said.

Tatum had politely refused. Then, after Ruth had continued pressing, Tatum, for once, stood her ground. It had felt good. Exhilarating. And, this came as a shock, Ruth had backed off. For the moment, Tatum told herself. Her trials with her ex-mother-in-law were probably far from over, but she'd made progress by setting some new ground rules.

"Can we get ice cream?" Gretchen had been asking the same question for the past few weeks, ever since Ryder had taken Tatum and the boys to Cascade's.

"Okay. On the way home."

Tatum relented not because of her daughter's persistence but because, after a difficult meeting with Lenny, she could probably use a little comfort food herself.

Gretchen's smile was short-lived. "Can Lisa Anne visit me in Mesa?"

"Of course. Once we're settled."

Leaving her best school chum was probably going to be the hardest of many adjustments for her daughter. Leaving Benjie would be the worst for Drew. Fortunately, Adam was too young to understand the full implications of his mother taking a new job and moving them—for the third time in less than a year—to a new place. One with a different school, different day care facility, different neighbors.

As she did every hour on the hour, Tatum wondered if she was making the right decision. It had seemed right at the time, now she was less sure. Ryder had called her reaction to Mercer's reprimand knee-jerk and impulsive. Perhaps he was right.

Just thinking his name filled her with regret. But she believed everything she'd said to him during their argument. Tatum couldn't enter into a committed relationship until she'd put her life in order. If not, she'd be depending on him to take care of her and the kids. She had already been down that road with Monty, and it wasn't a good one.

But, dear Lord, she missed Ryder. The past five days had dragged on forever. They'd seen each other at the arena. That couldn't be helped. Fortunately for her, their conversations were short and polite. Any longer, any more personal or intimate, and she'd surrender to the reconciliation he obviously wanted.

Parking in the small lot behind the store, Tatum and Gretchen entered through the back door. Tatum still had her key, which she intended to return to Lenny, along with an apology. She was leaving him in a bind.

They weren't the only ones in the store. In fact, all of Reckless was a bit busier than usual, probably because school had let out early today. Tatum had debated picking up the boys from day care, then opted not to. They would only distract her, and she needed to stay focused.

Signaling to Lenny that she would be in the art studio, Tatum hurried Gretchen along.

"Can I paint, Mommy?"

"Sure." Tatum quickly busied her daughter with paper and watercolors. She'd rather speak to Lenny alone, and, this way, Gretchen would be occupied and content.

While waiting for the store to empty, Tatum looked around the studio and located some card stock and markers. Sitting at one of the tables, she started creating a sign for the window announcing that the art studio was closing. Last evening, she'd made calls to her students' parents, advising them that classes would be canceled as of this weekend. They all expressed their disappointment and wished her luck in her new endeavors.

Tatum didn't get very far on the sign. By the third word, her eyes filled with tears. She'd miss this place and her classes. Almost as much as she'd miss her friends. She consoled herself with a reminder that she'd be teaching again, if only at a preschool.

During her short cry, the store emptied. "I'll be right back, sweetie pie," she told Gretchen. "You stay here while I talk to Mr. Faust."

Completely absorbed in her painting, Gretchen hardly noticed. Tatum had to smile. She'd been like that once, too, when she was young. Completely and utterly focused on her art.

Lenny offered her a big smile when she walked through the adjoining door. "It's not Saturday. What brings you by?"

"You have a minute?"

"Sounds serious." Lenny's smile didn't waver. He never assumed the worst and was always in good spirits.

Tatum went to the counter and stood across from him. Best to get right to the point. "I'm taking that job in Mesa. I'll be moving sooner than expected."

"How soon?"

"Next week." She could commute to the new job from Reckless, but only for a short time—and only if Cassidy agreed to pick up Gretchen and the boys every day after school. It really was a lot to ask, even of a best friend. Better to find a place quickly. "I'm sorry for having to break my lease early. I promise to have the space cleaned up before I leave, so you can look for a new tenant."

"No problem." Lenny shrugged one shoulder. "Truth is, I may have found another use for it."

"Really?" Interesting, since his rent was going up January first.

"Been talking to the manager at the bank. Interest rates on small business loans are low. Now's as good a time as any for me to borrow money and expand the store."

Tatum was bit flummoxed. He hadn't ever mentioned expanding the store before. "Is the shipping business that good?"

"It's steady. But I was actually thinking of adding a small office supply store. The pharmacy sells a few things. Envelopes and pens and such. If anyone wants a printer cartridge or masking tape or even paper clips, they have to drive into Globe."

How often had Tatum and her fellow teachers lamented the same thing?

"Might even sell some of that craft stuff you were always needing back when you were teaching."

A craft store. Tatum's silly dream that Ryder had said wasn't silly at all. Did she ever discuss her idea with Lenny? She couldn't remember. She must have. Or, Ryder did.

"Maggie Phillips was in here the other day complaining about needing poster board and markers," he said. "She was hoping to borrow some from you, but you weren't in the studio."

Tatum recalled running into Maggie outside the hardware store in Globe. She'd been on a supply run then, too.

She felt a pang deep in her heart. "I'm jealous of you, Lenny."

"Why?"

"The store. I've wanted to do something like that myself for years now."

Lenny's smile widened. "Come work for me."

"I didn't mean to," she sputtered.

"Can't do it all myself. I'd have to hire someone. Why not you? Unless you're set on that job in Mesa."

Tatum started to tell him yes, she was. The words, however, struck in her throat and refused to budge. She didn't want to move to Mesa. She didn't want to take a temporary position. She wanted to stay in Reckless. Her home.

"How much would the job pay?"

She had to be a realist and not get ahead of herself. Especially after all her talk about needing to grow up and make it on her own.

"Can't afford much to start." Lenny named an hourly wage. "I can see about a raise in a few months."

She could manage on that amount. If she watched her pennies very, very closely.

"Can I continue my art classes?" she asked, already thinking of adding evening classes to the schedule.

"Wouldn't have it any other way."

"Then I accept." She thrust her hand forward, and Lenny shook it gladly.

"Welcome aboard."

The decision felt right, much better than the temporary position at the preschool.

She'd have to call the agency right away. And tell Sunny and Cassidy. They would be glad for her and understand why she wasn't returning to the arena. Running a small office supply and craft store, continuing with her art lessons, was a much better fit for Tatum than working at the Easy Money.

And the kids! They'd be overjoyed. Tatum couldn't wait to tell them. That bigger house wasn't in their immediate plans. It might be if she worked hard and helped Lenny grow the business.

Ryder would be happy for her, too, she was certain. He'd be glad she was staying in Reckless.

Tatum felt another pang in her heart. The new job with Lenny put her one step closer to her goal of better managing her life on her own. But she still wasn't ready for a commitment. Maybe. One day. By then, Ryder would probably have met someone else. He was much too good-looking to go for long without attracting the attention of a woman. And he'd be at a new company, making new contacts on a daily basis.

"I'm meeting with a general contractor on Tuesday," Lenny said.

Tatum cleared her mind of Ryder and what couldn't be and concentrated on Lenny.

"I need a construction estimate to take to the bank before they'll start the loan paperwork. I don't think there needs to be a lot done to the space. Paint and flooring. Some shelves. The ceiling tile is shot. Stocking the merchandise is what'll cost the most."

"Have you ever considered selling teaching supplies? If not selling them, then having catalogues on hand that the teachers can order from? It would be easy enough to have the items shipped to the store."

"I like it." Lenny nodded thoughtfully.

They talked for several more minutes, hammering out details and brainstorming. Tatum forgot about the time.

"Mommy, how much longer?" Gretchen had come into the store.

Tatum went to her, picked her up and swung her in a circle. "Guess what, sweetie pie? We're not moving to Mesa! We're staying here, and Mommy's going to work for Mr. Faust."

Gretchen promptly broke into sobs, hiding her face in Tatum's tummy.

"What's wrong?"

"I can stay in school?"

Tatum stroked her daughter's hair. "Yes, and with all your friends."

Lenny offered them both tissues. It was only then that Tatum realized she, too, was crying. She dabbed Gretchen's cheeks and then her own.

"Let's get your painting," she told Gretchen, "and clean up. I have to pick up your brothers in an hour."

"Can I call Lisa Anne? Please."

Her classmate from school. How could Tatum say no? She handed Gretchen her cell phone. When Lisa Anne's mother offered to take Gretchen with them to the library, Tatum accepted, glad for a chance to continue working uninterrupted.

She and Lenny agreed to meet the following day for coffee and continue their discussion. She'd also attend the meeting he had scheduled with the general contractor.

After Gretchen left with her friend, Tatum made quick work of restoring order to the art studio. With a flourish, she tore up the partially completed sign and threw the bits into the wastebasket. Tomorrow, she'd make new signs. One advertising art classes and the other announcing the store's expansion.

She was just about to leave the studio when the bell above the front door jangled. Expecting to see a parent inquiring about the canceled lessons, or even Maggie needing classroom supplies, Tatum affixed a happy smile on her face and pivoted, ready to spread the good news.

Instead, Ryder walked toward her, his stride long and his expression that of a man with purpose.

"I WAS JUST LEAVING."

Ryder wasn't about to let Tatum off the hook that easily. "I won't keep you long." Just in case she attempted a quick escape, he edged closer.

She studied him up and down. "Are you blocking my way?"

"No." He didn't budge.

"Doesn't matter. I parked in the back."

Damn. He should have realized that when he didn't see her car out front.

"What do you want, Ryder?"

At first, he assumed she was still mad at him. All right, to be expected. He'd said some pretty stupid things to her last week. On second thought, that could be longing in her eyes. Or remorse. Or even uncertainty. Whichever, the fact she didn't demand he leave that instant gave him hope.

"This isn't a good time. Gretchen will be back any second, and I have to pick up the boys."

"Can I come by your apartment later?" he asked.

"We have plans."

Tatum had wavered for an instant before answering, giving Ryder even more hope.

Encouraged, he surged ahead. "I spoke to Lynda Spencer on the way into town. She committed to using Easy Money bucking stock for her next six rodeos. At the terms we originally agreed on."

Tatum's jaw went momentarily slack. "That's wonderful," she said when she recovered.

"We'll make good money. In the end."

"You have no idea how happy I am to hear that."

"No more than me." He paused. "You don't have to quit now."

"I do."

"This isn't me taking care of you, Tatum. The mistake was mine to fix."

"Actually, I agree." She reached for her purse. "But that changes nothing."

She was leaving. Ryder didn't have much time.

"I turned down the job at Velocity Concepts."

"You did?" She blinked in disbelief.

"I'm staying."

"You are?"

"I'd like to say I had an epiphany. What I had was a serious butt kicking from my dad. Seems he's a lot smarter than I gave him credit for. But don't tell him I said that."

"Your secret's safe with me." A hint of amusement lit her eyes.

For a second, she was the old Tatum. The one before their argument.

"Don't go," he blurted. "Stay in Reckless."

"Oh, Ryder." She was slipping away from him. He could feel it.

"I should have come home years ago," he said.

"Or, maybe you came home at just the right time. You've reconciled with your mother and joined the family business."

"I found you, too." This time, he didn't hold back his words. "And I shouldn't have let you go. I was wrong. I was stupid. I want a second chance."

"We can't just start over."

"Why not? Mesa isn't far."

"I'm not moving to Mesa."

"Not moving," he echoed dumbly.

"There's been a...a change," Tatum said.

"You're staying?"

Her glance went to the open door dividing the Ship-With-Ease Store from the art studio. Lenny stood behind the counter, assisting a customer. When she returned her gaze to Ryder, a smile pulled at the corners of her mouth.

"Lenny's expanding the store. To include office and craft supplies and even teaching supplies."

"Like you talked about."

Her smile widened, light and lovely. "He needs help and offered me a job assisting him. I'm still going to teach art, and—"

She didn't finish. She couldn't. Ryder left her speechless when he scooped her up in his arms.

"Ryder! Put me down." Her objection was weak at best, so he ignored it.

"Go out with me. Tonight. We'll celebrate. Dinner at the nicest restaurant in Globe."

"I already told you, I'm busy."

"Break your plans."

"Are you crazy?"

"I've been accused of worse."

"Really, Ryder. I'm serious."

He didn't believe her because she was laughing. The sound worked like a magic spell, enabling him to see the future clearly. It included his and Tatum's families joined together for always.

"Put me down." She pushed on his chest with the palms of her hands.

"I will." He gazed down at her. "As soon as you agree to marry me."

Tatum gasped. "You *are* crazy."

"I love you, Tatum." He kissed her then, not caring that customers in the Ship-With-Ease Store were staring at them. When he and Tatum broke apart, her cheeks were flushed. He liked her discombobulated.

"I can't marry you. Absolutely not. It's too soon."

So much for his father's theory that women needed a proposal. Well, at least she hadn't said she didn't love him. And she was still smiling.

"Then we'll date for a while. I think three months should be long enough. In the meantime, we'll find a house. One with four bedrooms. Or five. I can't stay in Dad's spare room any longer."

"Five bedrooms. That's a *huge* house."

"We have a big family." He gave her his best seductive grin. "Who knows? Could be even bigger one day."

She stared at him. "You want children?"

"I want your children. I'll be a good stepdad. And if we have one of our own, all the better."

"You're impossible." Her voice cracked with emotion.

Better than crazy. "I want to marry you, Tatum. When you're ready. When the time is right."

"I love you, too," she said, finally telling him what he desperately needed to hear. "I think I fell for you that first day, when you removed Cupcake's shoe in your dress clothes."

Before he could kiss her again, they were interrupted by Gretchen entering the studio.

She stood staring at them, her lower lip protruding in a severe pout. "I already have a daddy."

Ryder let go of Tatum and went to the girl. Kneeling in front of her, he took her by the shoulders. "I'm not going to take the place of your father. I promise you that. He's your dad and always will be. But I'm hoping we can be friends. Good friends. There isn't anything I want more."

She refused to look at him, so he tucked a finger beneath her chin and tilted her face to his.

"Your brothers like me. Do you think you could learn to like me, too? Even a little?"

"Will you take me to Cascades for ice cream?"

"Every weekend, if that's what you want."

"Okay, then."

Ah, the power of ice cream.

Ryder stood, his chest tight. He'd never been happier.

"Yes," Tatum said.

He looked at her, not sure he understood. "Yes, you'll have dinner tonight?"

"Yes, I'll marry you. When the time is right."

Wrong. He could indeed be happier.

Outside the studio, when Gretchen wasn't watching, he pulled Tatum into his arms and pressed his lips to hers for another satisfying kiss, promising himself that the next wedding in Reckless wouldn't be a pretend one. Theirs would be real and legal and the start of his and Tatum's lives together as husband and wife.

Ryder hadn't merely come home when he returned to Reckless. He'd found his true calling after years of wandering. No one was more surprised than him to discover the confirmed bachelor was really a family man at heart.

* * * * *

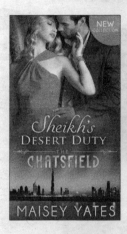

MILLS & BOON®

Seven Sexy Sins!

CATHY WILLIAMS
To Sin with the Tycoon

DANI COLLINS
The Sheikh's Sinful Seduction

The true taste of temptation!

From greed to gluttony, lust to envy, these fabulous stories explore what seven sexy sins mean in the twenty-first century!

Whether pride goes before a fall, or wrath leads to a passion that consumes entirely, one thing is certain: the road to true love has never been more enticing.

Collect all seven at
www.millsandboon.co.uk/SexySins